Snow Way Out

Alaska Cozy Mystery
Book 15

Wendy Meadows

Chapter One

Sarah was thrilled to be pregnant. Oh, her deepest and truest dream had become a sweet reality. Being pregnant was the closest thing to heaven on earth. Carrying a sweet, tender life inside of her womb was a gift—a treasure—an unimaginable joy that no words could ever give justice to. Yes, being pregnant with her very own tender, precious child was a gift from God above—a gift that Sarah would carry inside of her heart forever.

But being pregnant also had tiny little hardships. "Oh… I'm only four months pregnant, but I feel like a whale," Sarah moaned as she touched her belly.

Amanda grinned. "Love, you're barely showing. You have a little bump."

Sarah took a chocolate donut out of a Krispy Kreme box, scarfed it down, and smiled. "A little dramatic?" she asked.

"A tad." Amanda smiled back, took a donut for herself, and then laughed. "Wait until you're a full nine months, love…and then we'll talk."

"That's five months away…five little months." Sarah

beamed. "Just think, June Bug, in five months I'm going to be holding my child." Sarah stood up from the fancy wooden table and began walking around the luxury hotel room located in Los Angeles. The room, which had been paid for by Jill Nayforth, the woman who was currently in charge of making sure a new game show called *Pregnant Bliss* was going to see grand success, was soaked with every type of goodie a woman could dream of. Of course, Sarah thought as she walked over to a window covered with a soft green curtain, the room was designed to pamper and spoil women, and she had absolutely no problem with that. "In five months...just five little months."

Amanda watched Sarah pull back the curtain and look out at downtown Los Angeles. Bright, warm sunlight splashed onto Sarah, making the beautiful woman glow. Amanda watched as the sunlight dripped off of Sarah's golden hair and began dancing on a very stylish dark blue maternity dress. "You're at peace, love," she said in a grateful, loving tone.

Sarah studied the tall buildings of downtown Los Angeles, feeling as if she had walked back in time. The sun glittered off the buildings and rained down onto the crowded streets and sidewalks, soaking both the innocent and the guilty alike. The sight of the sun shining off the tall buildings was a familiar sight that never left Sarah's memory, but it was only part of the intense feeling. She turned her eyes west toward the Pacific, smiled, and then turned her eyes east—and even though she could barely see the canyons, she felt the dry, parched land inside of her heart.

"I miss Los Angeles," she told Amanda as she rotated her eyes back west and searched for the Pacific. "I miss the sights, the sounds, the way the sun splashes off the buildings, the canyons, the beaches, the crowded sidewalks…even the traffic."

Sarah slowly turned away from the window, closed the curtain, and focused on Amanda. Amanda, her sweetest, dearest friend in the world, was sitting at the fancy table holding a donut and wearing a dress that matched the donut. Oh, how Sarah loved and adored her sweet British friend.

"I miss what was…but I don't miss what is," she continued. "Los Angeles is a constantly changing city, June Bug. If I had never divorced my first husband, would I still be living here? Most likely, I suppose. I guess I would have never learned of Snow Falls, Alaska." Sarah sat back down at the table and found another donut. "I enjoy the city," she told Amanda in a relaxed voice. "And I'm happy to be back…on vacation, only. As much as Los Angeles—the memories, at least—is a part of me, I could never live in this city again."

"But it sure is fun to be on vacation and going on a nifty game show, right, love?" Amanda beamed and hurriedly reached for a Chick-Fil-A bag full of goodies.

"Well…in a way, I suppose." Sarah nodded. She picked up a cold bottle of water she had soaked with lemon juice, took a sip, and then continued. "Jill invited me to be a contestant because—"

"You killed the daughter of the Back Alley Killer, officially making you a star all over again…and officially ending the bloodline to that poisonous family," Amanda informed Sarah in a proud voice.

"I didn't exactly kill Lara," Sarah pointed out as Amanda fetched four chicken sandwiches and four boxes of waffle fries out of the Chick-Fil-A bag.

Amanda placed two sandwiches and two boxes of fries

before Sarah and then slid a delicious cookies 'n cream milkshake over to her friend. "Dig in, love."

Sarah bowed her head, said a prayer of thanks, and then reached for the milkshake. "I'm grateful that justice was served, June Bug. However, I wish people wouldn't see me as some kind of hero. Jesus is my hero."

Amanda retrieved her own milkshake. "People are grateful you are the winner, that's all. Enjoy the attention, because soon enough we're going to be back in our sleepy little Alaska town struggling through another harsh winter." Amanda glanced at the Krispy Kreme box and went for another donut. "A little sweet before the solids," she giggled.

Sarah grinned. Amanda was silly. "Our husbands are currently not present, so I guess it won't hurt to sneak down these donuts."

Amanda made an innocent face, walked her eyes around the room, and then giggled. "Come to momma," she told the donut and gobbled it down. Sarah laughed and handed Amanda a napkin. "Now it's time for the solids…maybe a little milkshake first?" Amanda waggled her eyebrows.

"I think I'm ready for dinner." Sarah laughed again and dived into a delicious chicken sandwich. "June Bug?" she said.

"Yes, love?" Amanda responded as she took down a sip of milkshake and then went for her waffle fries.

"Is this too good to be true?" Sarah asked. She swallowed a bite of food and then took down some of her milkshake. "I mean, I'm finally pregnant…the Snowman is dead…and look at us. We're…happy." Sarah looked Amanda deep in the eyes. "When we were at the hot springs…June Bug, I honestly thought our story had come to an end. A day like today would have seemed fantastical to even consider."

"I know what you mean." Amanda nodded. "We've dealt with some pretty ugly spiders, love. There were times when I thought the fog had finally rolled in for good." Amanda gobbled down a handful of waffle fries. "But look at us now, right? We're happy. My hubby is finally back—"

"And currently at Pete's office with Conrad," Sarah pointed out.

"That's right." Amanda smiled and then sighed. "Pete, he's such a doll. A grouch at times, but a doll. I love that old bear. I just hope my hubby can find common ground…" Amanda made a pained face. "Was it really smart to suggest he help Pete and Conrad track down a jewel thief?"

"I guess we'll find out," Sarah teased Amanda. "If Pete doesn't kill your hubby first, that is."

Amanda wrinkled her nose at Sarah. "Thanks a lot, love."

Sarah took another bite of her sandwich. "Oh, I wouldn't worry too much, June Bug. Pete is after a twenty-year-old female who takes jobs at local jewelry stores."

"And robs those stores when they close," Amanda added. "A pretty young girl who turns a man's brain into mush. If I remember correctly, this girl has robbed seven jewelry stores."

"She's a smart thief," Sarah agreed and went for her milkshake. "Constantly changing her appearance, has numerous fake identifications…real smart. However," Sarah emphasized, "she's not smart enough to escape Pete."

"Let's hope so," Amanda said and then decided to focus on a different subject. Her heart was sick of crime. "So, are you excited about tomorrow? You could win a ton of goodies."

"Well…I mean, the nursery back home is already complete," Sarah told Amanda in a thoughtful voice. "The prizes Jill is presenting on the show are items I already have—"

"But you don't have the grand prize," Amanda informed Sarah in an excited voice. "Love, you could win an all-expense-paid world cruise." Amanda clapped her hands together like a giddy schoolgirl. "Oh, a world cruise. You leave Florida, sail to the Caribbean Islands….down to Brazil…up to Europe…into the Mediterranean…Greece….Israel…and then it's off to Asia…Australia…oh, the romance…the smell of salty air…the sunsets…"

"In other words, you want me to win the cruise for you," Sarah giggled.

Amanda jumped up, ran to Sarah, dropped down onto her knees, and cried: "Please, oh please, I want to go on that cruise! Please win for me…do it for your little English muffin…please, love…oh please!"

Sarah laughed, took Amanda's hands, and promised: "I will do my best, June Bug. Even if I fail…I'll buy you a world cruise."

"No can do, love," Amanda sighed. "You know my hubby. Making that man go on vacation is like pulling teeth, as you Americans say." Amanda rolled her eyes. "He will never go on a cruise unless he pays for it, and although we have money, he's still a crummy tightwad. It's a wonder I love him." Amanda snapped her arms together and made a clever little face. "But love, if you win that cruise…oh…and present it as a prize…oh, I just know I can talk my hubby into packing his seasick pills."

"Seasick pills?" Sarah laughed.

Amanda grinned. "For better or worse includes seasickness —which means while my hubby is hugging the toilet I can shop until I drop."

Sarah put her hand over her face and laughed. "You're a

very devious woman—" She stopped when the room door opened. Conrad appeared with a very angry expression on his face. "Honey?"

Conrad snatched off his leather jacket and threw it down onto the king-sized bed covered with a soft blue blanket. "I like Pete. He's a good cop and a good man and a good friend and all of that jazz," Conrad exploded in a voice that could have strangled thin air. He marched over to the table, grabbed one of Amanda's chicken sandwiches, and then went back to the bed and sat down. "A man has his limits, Sarah…"

Sarah watched Conrad take an angry bite out of the chicken sandwich he stole from Amanda. "What did Pete, do, honey?"

"It's what that man didn't do," Conrad fussed. "There we were, all set to snatch up a woman we believed to be the jewel thief…and do you know what Pete did?"

"What?" Amanda asked in a pained voice. "And please tell me my hubby isn't as mad as you are…oh please…oh please."

Conrad rolled his eyes. "My dear and close friend from Alaska is still with Pete, dining at Pete's favorite Chinese restaurant."

"Honey, what did Pete do to make you so upset?" Sarah asked in a concerned voice. It was rare that Pete and Conrad were ever at odds with one another.

"He didn't snatch the girl, that's what Pete didn't do," Conrad informed Sarah and tore another bite of sandwich loose. "He contradicted me right in front of Amanda's better half." Conrad stood up, marched back to the table, and swiped Sarah's milkshake. "The evidence was clear. We had the girl in our sights. But no, Pete decided it was better to wait. For what? I'll tell you what!" Conrad took down some milkshake, set the cup down, and then grabbed some waffle fries. "Pete believes it will be smarter if we wait until the girl manages to snag a gig at another jewelry store. Yeah, that's exactly what we need…another robbed store."

Sarah studied Conrad's angry face. Conrad wasn't mad at Pete. "Honey?" she said in a careful voice. "Are you really mad at Pete or Andrew?" she asked. "I mean, forgive me for taking Pete's side, but Pete is in charge of the case and his plan does hold merit."

Conrad glanced down at Sarah's beautiful face and then walked back to the bed and plopped down. "Don't mention that guy's name to me, Sarah. As far as I'm concerned, Andrew is no longer a friend." Conrad rubbed his eyes and let out an irritated groan. "Yeah, I know Pete was right, okay?" he confessed.

Amanda made a confused face. "Did I miss something, love?"

Sarah sighed, touched her tender belly, and then decided to tell Amanda all about the falling out Conrad and Andrew had suffered four days earlier. "Conrad arrested a woman who is close friends with Andrew's wife…a Mrs. Mintstone—"

"The woman slapped me," Conrad jumped in. "She entered the diner drunk as a skunk and began disrupting the peace."

"Mrs. Mintstone is self-medicating her…uh…depression," Sarah added in a voice that she hoped didn't sound disrespectful. The thought of a woman living in a small Alaska town getting toasted every day because her husband had decided to finally admit he didn't like the woman's cooking… after twenty years of marriage…wasn't exactly a disaster.

"Depression…that's a laugh," Conrad huffed. "The woman

is upset because her husband has finally come right out and said her meatloaf stinks like rotten eggs."

"Really?" Amanda gasped. "I know Mrs. Mintstone. That woman is very…well, temperamental over her cooking." Amanda made a "golly" face. "My goodness."

"Well," Conrad told Amanda, "to make a long story short, I arrested Mrs. Mintstone for assault. But Andrew, that crumb, released her and tossed the charge into the waste basket— while I was at home eating dinner with my wife, that is."

"Honey, I admit what Andrew did was wrong," Sarah told her furious husband, "but you have to look at it from his point of view."

"Yeah, I know," Conrad cut Sarah off. "Andrew's wife threatened to make him sleep in the doghouse if he didn't drop the charge. But that's…Sarah, a woman assaulted me… broke the law…and Andrew trampled all over the law. That's what angers me the most…that crumb bag."

"We do live in a small town," Sarah pointed out. "Andrew does have his life and family to consider, honey. He has other friends besides us."

"Andrew is supposed to be a cop first. If he can't be a cop and uphold the law, the guy needs to put his badge away." Conrad stood up, looked around the room, and shook his head. "I'm going for a walk," he said. He hurried over to Sarah, kissed her tummy, and then stormed out of the room.

"Well," Amanda whispered in a shocked voice, "I would have never assumed in a million years…I mean, Andrew and Conrad are best friends."

"Looks like we have a storm to face when we return home," Sarah told Amanda and then grabbed her milkshake. "In the meantime, let's eat. My baby needs food." Sarah drank some milkshake and smiled. She wasn't so worried about Conrad and Andrew's little falling out. In the end, Sarah knew, Andrew was going to make things right; or so she hoped. In the meantime, she had a game show to think about and a world cruise to win.

Chapter Two

Lights. Cameras. Studio audience. A large studio filled with different stages holding games and prizes. Yes, *Pregnant Bliss* was officially prepared to host its debut show.

"Okay, Sarah," Jill Nayforth said in a nervous voice as she chewed on a piece of strawberry licorice like a dog chewing on a bone. "Here are the rules—"

"Jill, I already know—" Sarah tried to speak as a lovely young makeup artist tended to her beautiful face. Sarah felt cramped and trapped in the expensive, brightly lit dressing room Jill had assigned her. The dressing room might as well have been a small mansion as far as Sarah was concerned. And the dress…oh, Jill had insisted that Sarah wear a bright pink maternity dress that made Sarah look like a whale. Not that Sarah minded the color pink, and she certainly loved dresses— but a large bright pink whale dress…oh dear. And her hair… Jill had insisted Sarah wear her hair in a tight "mommy" bun. Sarah felt as if she had been turned into a silly clown.

"Listen," Jill cut Sarah off, pacing back and forth behind

the black leather chair Sarah was sitting on like a panicked cat, "the rules are simple. Leah Mayes will ask you a series of questions. For each question you get right you get to play a game, and in return, depending on how you play the game, you may win or lose a prize. Now, the questions are simple, and the games are not difficult."

Jill stopped talking, reached into the pocket of the brown leather jacket she was wearing even though the day was extremely warm, and yanked out another piece of licorice. Sarah shook her head at the stressed woman but didn't speak. Instead, she studied Jill's middle-aged face that wasn't beautiful or ugly but simply average, if a bit bony. Jill Nayforth, Sarah clearly understood, was a woman who worked long, difficult hours to please money-hungry television people who didn't care that Jill had suffered an ugly divorce and had lost over forty pounds.

"Sarah, we have to draw a major female audience and you are the magnet. There isn't a sensible woman in this country that doesn't see you as her hero." Jill placed a nervous hand on Sarah's shoulder. "You're my big star, okay?" she said, dropping into a pep talk tone of voice. "Leah has been given a series of questions that we know you can answer and—"

"What?" Sarah quickly brushed the makeup artist away. "Jill, I didn't travel to Los Angeles to cheat," she exclaimed.

Jill quickly put a finger over Sarah's mouth. "Cheat… Sarah, no," she whispered, tossing a quick, stern eye at the makeup artist. The young woman shrugged her shoulders and left the dressing room. She had better things to do with her time than deal with two old bats. "Listen, all I did was…tweak the questions a little," Jill continued as Sarah removed her hand. "We can't risk you losing the spotlight."

Sarah wanted to be angry at Jill for deceiving her. Instead, she looked into a panicked face that she pitied. Jill was on the verge of a major nervous breakdown. Pushing the woman into a corner wasn't a good idea. Besides, Amanda did want a world cruise, and what would it hurt to play along with Jill's plan? Television was television.

"I'll answer the questions that I'm asked to the best of my knowledge," she promised Jill. "But don't tell me what the questions are."

A relieved smile washed across Jill's face. "Don't worry, Sarah, the questions I have in store for you are simple, basic questions that you will have no problem answering." Jill quickly checked her short, curly black hair and then looked at the time on her fancy silver cell phone. "Oh dear…we have less than ten minutes," she exclaimed. "Sarah, darling…oh dear." Jill quickly grabbed Sarah's arm, yanked the poor woman to her feet, and ran her out of the dressing room and down a long hallway covered with expensive green carpet. "Okay, when Leah announces your name," she explained, "and when you hear the music begin to play, that's when you walk out onto the stage."

"I understand," Sarah assured Jill. "We've been through this numerous times, Jill. I know my part."

Jill dragged Sarah through a wooden door that led to a large, open backstage that was full of people buzzing around. The long, thick, blue and pink stage curtain separated the backstage from the main stage. "Stand here," Jill ordered Sarah, marching her over to the side of the curtain and placing her inside of a blue and pink box that had been painted on the floor. "When you hear your name—"

"And when the music starts to play—"

"And when that light turns green," Jill informed Sarah and pointed to a green light attached to the side of the stage wall.

"I understand," Sarah promised.

Jill studied Sarah's lovely face and then forced a nervous smile to her own thin, bony face. "Let's make this happen, Sarah," she begged and then hurried off into the shadows of the backstage to run one last errand before the show started.

Sarah shook her head, sighed, and peeked her head forward around the edge of the heavy stage curtain. She spotted a fancy blue and white carpet surrounded by a room that resembled a large baby nursery built for adults. A redheaded woman wearing a blue and pink onesie was approaching a wooden stand that had been turned into a large alphabet block. A single white chair sat next to the wooden stand. The chair faced a studio audience composed of mostly happy pregnant women…and a very anxious Amanda.

"No need to be nervous, sweet baby," Sarah whispered and patted her tender tummy. "Mommy is simply going to play a game. We're going to have fun and win all kinds of prizes."

The redheaded woman—Leah Mayes—quickly stepped behind the wooden block and picked up a black microphone as overhead speakers began to play "Rock-a-Bye Baby" in a rock 'n roll tune that Sarah didn't care for. A green light stationed above the curtain began to flash, signaling the studio audience to start clapping.

"Hello, everyone. My name is Leah Mayes, and let me be the first to welcome all of you to…" Leah paused for effect and threw her wild arms up into the air, "Pregnant Bliss, the only game show where soon-to-be mothers are given the chance to win fabulous prizes for their little pie in the oven!"

"Oh, good grief," Sarah moaned, disappointed to see a hip,

modern game show forming before her eyes instead of a traditional, warm, fun game show that would have made the 1950s shine. "What did I get myself into?"

"And now, ladies, let's have some fun!" Leah yelled as if she were at a rock concert listening to music that rots a person's brain. "Rock-a-Bye Baby" quickly morphed into some kind of horrific intro full of electric guitars that sounded as if they were dying. "Our first contestant is no stranger to the limelight," Leah spoke into the microphone. "Please, ladies, put your hands together for Detective Sarah Garland!"

Sarah rolled her eyes and stepped out onto the bright stage. She was greeted by waves of cheers from pregnant women who were mostly in their twenties. Poor Amanda was sitting in the bottom row stuffed between two pregnant women who looked ready to deliver at any second. She raised a painful hand and waved at Sarah. Sarah grinned and then looked at Leah. "I'm happy to be here," she said.

"And we're excited to have you, aren't we, ladies!" Leah yelled in a wild voice and then hurried Sarah over to her seat as a red light appeared over the stage.

All the women sitting in the studio audience spotted the light and quickly stopped cheering and clapping. Poor Amanda tried to clear her aching ears. Was she at a game show or a rock concert? What in the world happened to nice, cozy —quiet—family game shows? Blimey Americans.

"Now Sarah," Leah spoke, stepping behind the wooden block, "although we know all about you, there may be some women with us today or watching from home who are not aware of who you are. Why don't you take a second to tell us about yourself?"

"Well—" Sarah began to speak.

"Detective Sarah Garland is the woman who took out a very cruel killer," Leah cut Sarah off, speaking in a spooky, creepy voice. "Sarah singlehandedly took out the Back Alley Killer, a monster who terrorized the city of Los Angeles. But was that enough? No." Leah glanced off stage and saw Jill give her a thumbs-up. "The daughter of the Back Alley Killer went after Sarah…and Sarah put her lights out." Leah pointed at Sarah. "We have a genuine hero sitting before us, ladies!" she yelled. "Give it up for Detective Sarah Garland!"

Sarah watched the studio audience go wild, sighing and waiting for the madness to end. "Actually," she quickly spoke before Leah could continue, "I'm retired, and my married name is Sarah Spencer."

"Fair enough," Leah said and quickly scooped up a piece of paper holding a set of questions. Leah Mayes couldn't have cared two cents for Sarah. All Leah Mayes cared about was her career. Hosting a crummy game show wasn't tops, but it was a start—and a lot better than walking down crummy runways working as a model. Leah was pushing thirty and the sand in the hourglass was draining fast.

"Okay, Sarah," she said, staying in character, "as great as it is to have you as our very first contestant, I'm afraid I can't break any rules for you. And speaking of rules, here they are!" Leah quickly explained all the rules of the show and then smiled at a set of cameras being operated by bored workers who were anxious for lunch. "Stay with us, ladies, because after a brief message from our sponsors, we're going to get the train moving!"

Sarah watched a man in his early sixties—who was dressed like a nineteen-year-old punk—wave his hands at Leah. "We're clear for five," he yelled. The makeup artist who had tended to Sarah quickly ran out onto the stage and hurried to Leah.

Leah closed her eyes as if she had worked eight long and stressful hours and allowed the makeup artist to fix her face. Sarah shrugged her shoulders at Amanda. Amanda shrugged back, then reached into her pink purse, took out a Tootsie Roll Pop, and began to open it.

"Oh, a Tootsie Roll Pop." The pregnant woman sitting next to Amanda beamed and snatched the candy pop out of Amanda's hands. Sarah watched her friend's face turn to shock and then sadness. Poor dear.

"Okay, here we go!" a voice yelled.

Leah quickly pushed the makeup artist away and hurried back to her station. As soon as the sixty-year-old punk gave her a thumbs-up, Leah shot back into character. "Okay, ladies, we're back and ready to rock!" she yelled in her wild voice. "Sarah, are you ready to play *Pregnant Bliss*?"

"Uh…sure." Sarah forced a weak smile to her face as Amanda dug out a second Tootsie Roll Pop. The pregnant woman sitting to her right quickly stole it. Amanda threw her hands up, then folded her arms and made a pouty face. Show business stunk.

"Okay, Sarah, I'm going to ask you a question, and if you answer the question correctly, we're going to play a game called Diaper Rash." Leah waited as two lovely women dressed in blue and white onesies pushed what appeared to be a board covered with white diapers attached to it. Each diaper had red numbers attached to them. "One of those diapers, Sarah, holds diaper rash medicine. It's up to you to find the right diaper." Leah's face suddenly grew very serious. "If you answer the question I'm about to ask you, Sarah, you will earn five points. Each point will allow you one guess as to which diaper holds the diaper rash medicine. But beware. One single diaper is full of…shall we say…poop! If you choose that diaper…you get covered."

"Covered?" Sarah gulped.

Leah nodded as two more lovely women pushed a large bucket of chocolate pudding onto the stage. "Let's hope you find the right diaper, Sarah," Leah announced, "because if you do, you will win…" Leah paused for effect, "a lovely new crib. Jake?"

A man's voice came over the speakers, speaking in a perky "advertisement" voice. The voice quickly spoke about the crib and what company the crib belonged to and blah, blah, blah as far as Sarah was concerned. All Sarah cared about was the large bucket of pudding. Jill had not mentioned anything about getting covered with pretend baby poop.

"Sarah, are you ready for your first question?" Leah asked.

"Uh…sure." Sarah tensed up a little. "This is just for fun," she whispered, "just for fun, little baby…fun."

"Sarah, here is your first question," Leah stated, turning serious again. "In what year did Sherlock Holmes make his first official appearance?"

Although Leah presented the question in an overeager "hip" tone instead of a traditional, intelligent manner, Sarah understood the question and knew the answer. But before she could respond, Leah suddenly, as if something had exploded in front of her eyes, threw her hands over her face and began screaming, shocking Sarah and everyone present.

"My face…it's burning…" Leah cried out in pain and tried to run off stage. Sarah shot to her feet and followed after her. Leah managed to make it behind the back curtain and then collapsed down onto the hardwood floor, where, to Sarah's horror, she breathed her last breath.

"Someone call nine-one-one!" Sarah yelled as she dropped down onto her knees and began to examine Leah. The woman's face was no longer lovely or beautiful. Leah's face was now…horrible.

When Amanda heard Sarah yell, she jumped to her feet and ran backstage. "Love?" she yelled, spotting Sarah leaning over Leah.

Jill burst past Amanda and raced over to Sarah. "I called nine-one-one. Is she…dead?"

Sarah grabbed Leah's left wrist and checked for a pulse. "No pulse…and I don't think it's possible to do CPR," she told Jill in a tragic, sorrowful voice, pointing to Leah's face. Jill looked down at the game show host's horrid face, nearly fainted, and then rushed away, leaving Amanda standing next to Sarah feeling confused and frightened. Show business certainly stunk like rotten eggs.

Chapter Three

The lights went off. Women screamed. The men who were present—most of whom were more frightened than the women—all scrambled away like rats deserting a ship. Hundreds of cell phones began to glow, being used as flashlights. Frantic voices filled the air as terrified women began calling their husbands—terrified women who were bumping into each other like intoxicated drivers searching for an off-ramp.

Sarah wanted to plead for calm, but the women, the majority of whom were pregnant, were too terrified to listen to reason. All Sarah could do was pull out her gun and stay with the dead body as Amanda whipped out her cell phone and turned it on.

"Love?" she said, flashing the cell phone down at Sarah's alert face.

"Stay calm, June Bug," Sarah whispered, resting on one knee with her gun at the ready as her eyes watched the glow of cell phones start fading away, leaving a deafening silence in the studio. "Jill?" she called out. "Jill, speak to me." Jill Nayforth didn't answer Sarah.

"I'm here." A strange and creepy voice slithered out from the darkness. "Don't try to leave the studio. I have three bombs. If you try to leave, the bombs will explode. I'm allowing everyone to leave except you, your friend, and three others."

Goosebumps ran down Sarah's spine. She quickly searched the darkness but could barely see past her own nose. "What do you want?" she called out.

"I have people watching the exits. When everyone is out, the game begins," the voice promised Sarah and then vanished into the dark womb of the studio.

Amanda quickly squatted down, keeping her eyes away from Leah's body, and looked at Sarah. "Are we cursed, love?" she asked in a miserable voice. "We're supposed to be enjoying a pregnant game show…blimey." Amanda placed her hand over her face. "I'm never leaving Snow Falls again…no world cruise. I'll spend the rest of my days shopping at O'Mally's, cleaning him out of kosher chili dogs."

"Sounds good to me," Sarah whispered, "but first we have to figure out what's going on, June Bug." Sarah grabbed Amanda's cell phone and called Conrad, waking the man up from a light sleep. He picked up on the fourth ring.

"We have trouble," Sarah spoke in an urgent voice.

"Are you okay? The baby isn't hurt is he…or she? Where are you?" Conrad asked as his eyes struggled to wake up. He jumped to his feet like a panicked husband expecting his wife to give birth at any second and looked for his gun. "I'm on my way…just stay calm…what's your location…"

"I'm at the studio," Sarah whispered, walking her eyes

around the darkness, searching for any signs of light or movement. "A woman is dead…somebody has planted three bombs…I can't leave." Sarah eased her voice down even lower. "Whoever is hiding in the shadows has let everyone leave except for me, Amanda, and three others. I don't know who the other three people are."

Conrad grabbed his gun off the nightstand, tossed it into the shoulder holster he was wearing, and then went for his shoes. "I'll get Pete on the phone…just stay calm."

"I'm calm," Sarah promised. "The cops have already been notified…" Sarah bit down on her lip. It was clear to her mind that whoever was hiding in the shadows—and there could possibly be more than one person—allowed the cops to be notified. But for what reason? And why was Leah Mayes targeted? "Conrad, I'm at studio A-17. It's a large airport hangar–type building sitting on the back lot of the Sun Waves Studio."

"I'm on my way," Conrad promised as he threw on his shoes and then ran for his leather jacket. "I'll get Pete moving."

"Have Pete run a woman named Leah Mayes," Sarah whispered. "Leah Mayes was the host of the game show. She's the dead woman." Sarah glanced over at Amanda, saw her worried friend searching the darkness, and then dared to look down at Leah's body. "Some type of skin poison was used to kill her—at least that's how it appears."

Conrad began to run out of the hotel room and then remembered his wallet and the room key. He dashed back to the nightstand, grabbed the two items, and then charged away. "Makeup?" he asked.

"She was killed after the show took a five-minute

commercial break. The show is being aired live and…" Sarah paused. "The show was being aired live…"

"Sarah?" Conrad asked as he snatched open the hotel room door and ran out into a long, lush hallway lined with closed doors.

"I'm here," Sarah assured him. "Conrad, get the bomb squad on the scene…" Again, Sarah felt her mind pause. Why had the killer…or killers…allowed the cops to be called? Why had the lights been doused after the fact? Why had the voice explained that three bombs were present? Sure, confessing the presence of three bombs was enough to make any person freeze in their tracks, but Sarah felt that there was a hidden reason. *And why force only five people to remain?* she asked herself.

"I'm moving," Conrad promised. "Stay calm…and don't let anything happen to our baby…or yourself. We're a family. You, me, and our baby makes three…" Conrad felt panic and pain strike his heart. What if something happened to Sarah and the baby? How would he continue to live? Life would crash to a horrible end. "I'm calling Pete right now and then I'll call you back."

Sarah heard Conrad end the call, handed Amanda back the cell phone, and glanced around. "Turn off the light," she whispered.

"Love?" Amanda said in an uncertain tone.

"Go dark," Sarah insisted.

Amanda had no desire to be in the dark with a dead body…but she completely trusted Sarah. "Okay." Amanda extinguished the light on her cell phone, allowing a heavy curtain of darkness to engulf her. "Now what?" she whispered.

Sarah handed Amanda her gun and then used the darkness

to hide her objective. She knew that Leah was wearing a different set of clothing under the costume onesie. She unzipped the onesie and felt what appeared to be a silk blouse. Below the silk blouse Sarah found a pair of jeans. Sarah quickly began checking the pockets of the jeans. She located a tube of lipstick, a pack of matches, and a folded-up piece of paper.

"That's all," she whispered, shoving the three items into the front pocket of her dress. She zipped the onesie back up and looked over at Amanda, barely able to see her silhouette in the dark. "Let's move…give me my gun and your hand."

"We can't leave, love…the bombs," Amanda whispered in a shaky voice.

"We're not leaving. Come on." Sarah took her gun back and then grabbed Amanda's hand. Using her mind rather than her eyes, she began crawling away from Leah. "It's so dark… but I know where we're at and I know the way back to the dressing room," she whispered, crawling over a hardwood floor that felt very rough on her knees. "The exit door is to our right."

"Why are we going to the dressing room?" Amanda asked, wincing at the roughness of the hardwood floor as her knees made one daring step after another.

"I have a feeling that's where I'm expected."

"Expected?" Amanda gulped.

Sarah nodded as she crawled toward the exit door, holding her gun in one hand and Amanda's hand in the other. "Yes," she whispered. "I believe—" Sarah's voice crashed to a halt when she saw the light of a cell phone light up near the exit door.

"Very good, Detective," a scary voice announced. "Go to

the dressing room with your friend and join the others. You will receive further instructions when you arrive."

Whoever was standing in the darkness was using some type of voice-altering device to hide his or her voice. Sarah couldn't discern whether the voice belonged to a man or a woman. She needed to play it smart. "The police and bomb squad are—"

"Yes, I know," the voice informed Sarah without a hint of concern. "Everything is working out as planned. Now, drop your gun and do as told."

Sarah watched as the shadowy person raised the cell phone light up to a face covered with a creepy clown mask. The mask didn't bother Sarah, but the night vision goggles covering the eyes of the clown mask did. The person standing near the exit door had eyes to see in the darkness—she didn't. "Who are you?"

"Do as told," the person ordered Sarah and slowly raised a right hand that was holding a Glock 17. "I will kill your friend if you refuse."

Sarah watched the shadowy figure aim the gun directly at Amanda. She was in a position to get off a clear shot and save her friend...but then what? What if she killed the strange clown—would the hidden bombs erupt? Were there more scary clowns hiding in the darkness like hungry monsters? Sarah knew she had to play the scene smart—real smart.

"Okay," she called out. She placed her gun down onto the hardwood floor and pushed it away into the hungry darkness.

"Perfect," the voice said and placed Amanda back into the clear. "Now, stand up and walk. I will lead the way. If you try any funny business...well..."

"Don't," a second voice spoke from behind Sarah. The

second voice, like the first one, was also using a voice-altering device. "The building is clear, and each exit door is now secure."

"Excellent." The shadowy figure standing in front of Sarah grinned. "Secure my back while I get these two to the dressing room."

"Let's move," Sarah whispered to Amanda, helping her friend stand up. They carefully approached the exit door, and then Sarah dared to glance over her shoulder. Intense darkness roamed the air. Whoever the second person was, Sarah knew, he or she was wearing night vision goggles, too.

"Follow me, ladies," the shadowy figure ordered.

"Show business stinks, love," Amanda grumbled under her breath as she stepped through the exit door with Sarah. A long, dark hallway greeted her eyes. Only the single light of a cell phone, glowing in the dark like a strange alien torch, allowed any illumination. "I'm never leaving Snow Falls ever, ever again."

Sarah squeezed Amanda's hand as she followed the light of the cell phone. The stranger leading the way had ordered Sarah to dispose of her gun…but not Amanda's cell phone. Why? She decided to ask as her legs walked past one closed door after another. "Why are you allowing us to keep our cell phones?"

The shadowy monster leading Sarah and Amanda back to Sarah's dressing room stopped walking. "You'll see, Detective. Sometimes props are needed to make a good show."

Sarah soaked in the person's words and began walking again. A few minutes later, she arrived at a closed door. "Inside," the person covering the rear ordered Sarah and Amanda.

Sarah watched the shadowy creature standing in front of her douse the cell phone he or she was holding and vanish into the darkness. "Come on, June Bug," she whispered as she opened the door leading into her dressing room and walked inside. Amanda quickly followed as a hard hand slammed the dressing room door closed behind her, causing the poor woman to nearly jump out of her skin.

"Sarah?" Jill called out, using the light of her cell phone to search the dressing room.

"Yes, it's me, Jill. My friend Amanda is with me," Sarah answered, spotting the lights of three cell phones glowing in the air. "Who is with you…everyone call out," she ordered in a tough cop voice. "Now!"

"Ryan Mables," a confused voice spoke into the air.

"Patty Darling," another voice spoke—a voice Sarah recognized. "I'm the makeup artist who was working on you… and Leah."

Sarah moved to the vanity she had been sitting at and scrambled around for her purse. Had the scary clown and his…or her…circus team captured her purse? Relief struck Sarah when her hands struck the lovely handbag Amanda had bought her as a gift. She quickly reached inside it and located her cell phone—and a hidden gun. Without wasting a second, Sarah turned her back to the three people standing close to her and checked the gun. "Still loaded," she whispered as she bent down and tucked the gun into a hidden ankle holster.

"Can someone tell me what's going on?" Ryan Mables asked. Ryan, who had just turned twenty-three four days prior to the live filming of the game show, was engaged to the lovely Patty Darling, the makeup artist. Ryan's mother, Cecilia Mables, despised Patty and forbid her son to marry the girl.

Cecilia Mables was an extremely wealthy divorcee who cherished her son but loathed the fact that he wanted to… ugh…marry Patty Darling, a sneaky little gold digger. "One minute Patty and I were heading toward the exit, and the next I had a gun in my face."

"Me, too," Patty added in a shaky voice. "Sarah, do you know what is happening?" Then she whispered to Ryan, "Your mother is behind this, I just know it. She hates me."

"My mother didn't kill Leah Mayes," Ryan answered his angry fiancée. As much as Ryan loved Patty, he never stopped defending Cecilia Mables. After all, the woman was his mother —a mother who loved her son very deeply. "My mother is in Italy right now visiting her sister."

"You always defend…that woman," Patty snapped at Ryan. She pulled away from his hands and used the cell phone in her hands to locate Sarah. "You're the famous cop…I suppose you think I killed Leah Mayes, huh?" she asked in a sour voice.

"You could have." Sarah nodded, saving the battery in her own cell phone. "Anyone standing in this room could be the killer."

"Sarah!" Jill gasped in shock. "I didn't kill—"

"I didn't say you killed Leah Mayes, Jill," Sarah quickly cut the frantic woman off. "I said anyone standing in this room could be a killer. Then again, whoever is holding us captive could have killed Leah Mayes. What I do know is that Leah was alive until Patty arrived and tended to her face during the commercial break."

"Yeah, sure, blame me," Patty snapped. "I'm just a stupid makeup artist, right?" Patty turned away from Sarah, turned off her cell phone, shoved it into the pocket of the green leather jacket she was wearing over a gray dress, and then ran her hands through long, black hair that had recently been styled to look messy and grunge-like, a style Sarah didn't like. "Blame the makeup artist," Patty finished in a sour tone as she found a chair and sat down. "After all, I'm just a miserable gold digger, right, Ryan?"

Sarah glanced at Amanda, who simply eased closer to her dear friend and waited for the lights to come on…or stay off. Yes, show business stunk like rotten eggs.

Chapter Four

"What?" Sarah asked Conrad, unsure if she had heard her husband correctly.

Conrad was standing outside of Studio A-17 amidst a crowd of cops, bomb squad personnel, firefighters, curious studio employees, and other assorted people who had gathered to see what all the commotion was. He glanced up at blue sky that was quickly growing gray and dark; a storm was approaching.

"I can barely hear you over all the noise," he screamed into his cell phone as a group of cops charged past him like soldiers rushing into battle. Conrad had no idea why the group of cops were charging at the studio with their guns drawn while a group of studio employees—actors still dressed in costume— were standing close by chatting away on their cell phones. The studio building, a large hangar-type structure that appeared big enough to swallow three aircraft carriers, stood over Conrad like a dark, imposing, hideous grin.

"Did you say this event is being broadcast?" Sarah asked

Conrad, standing in the far corner of the dressing room, speaking in a low voice.

"All over social media," Conrad yelled over the sound of an approaching fire truck that had its sirens blaring. The scene outside the studio was chaotic, if not circuslike. Unarmed civilians were peppered among armed cops who were aiming their guns at the studio, making the cops appear plain silly, if not downright stupid. Firefighters were rushing about like ants that had no true mission. Bomb squad personnel were wandering here and there, studying the studio like lost gnats dipping at a bit of sweat here and there. No one had a clue what to do except…do something that appeared useful and productive.

"Whoever is inside with you began broadcasting the show after the first commercial break."

"When Leah Mayes died."

Conrad shoved a finger into his left ear to drown out the sound of the approaching fire truck. "Yeah…looks that way," he yelled, spotting Pete pushing through the crowd wearing his gray overcoat, an old gray fedora, and a tough face. "Pete's here."

Pete stormed up to Conrad with a half-smoked cigar in his mouth. "I can't get answers from anyone," he fussed and then reached for Conrad's phone. Conrad nodded and surrendered the phone. "Kiddo?"

"Hey, Pete," Sarah whispered, barely able to hear Pete's voice over all the commotion taking place outside of the studio. "Amanda and I are okay."

"I don't know what loser is behind this," Pete informed Sarah, "but whoever it is—"

"There's more than one person involved, Pete," Sarah told

him, hoping her voice wasn't being heard by the people holding her captive. "I've encountered two people…one was wearing a creepy clown mask and a pair of night vision goggles."

"There's only one person broadcasting the show taking place inside," Pete responded. "Do you have internet on your phone?"

"Yes." Sarah tapped her screen and quickly brought up a popular social media site. Sarah personally didn't have a social media account—she loathed social media sites—but knew Amanda did in order to keep up with some old friends in London. "June Bug, what's your login?"

Amanda, who was standing mere inches away from Sarah, glanced down at the woman's cell phone. "Hold on, love," she whispered into her own cell phone, putting her frantic husband on hold, and whispered her username and password to Sarah.

Sarah quickly logged on and was immediately greeted by tons of news flashes concerning the murder of Leah Mayes and the capture of Studio A-17 by what appeared to be a crazed terrorist calling him or herself "Clown." Each news article had a link that took Sarah to Clown's social media page, where the monster was live streaming the event. Currently Clown was sitting in a lavish office that was dimly lit with candles speaking to an audience that consisted of millions of people.

"Stay tuned, because the game is going to begin very soon," Clown spoke, still utilizing the voice-altering device. "We have five contestants…one is the killer," Clown assured the watching audience. "If the other four contestants locate the real killer…no boom. If they fail…Los Angeles will be lit up tonight. And for the watchful eye of the law…remember, I have eyes everywhere. If anyone dares try to enter my studio… boom."

Sarah stared at the hideous clown mask the person speaking was wearing and struggled to decide if her eyes were seeing a man or a woman. Clown was sitting behind a desk with his or her hands clasped together. The hands were lathered in shadows and a pair of black gloves, making it impossible to spot any physical signs that pointed to a biological sex; fingernail polish, wedding band, fake fingernails, chewed fingernails. And, to make matters worse, Clown was wearing what appeared to be a black cloak.

"Who are you?" Sarah whispered.

Clown checked the viewer count attached to the social media page broadcasting the event. "We're almost to ten million. Whenever we reach that count the show will begin, ladies and gentlemen. So gather your friends, families, and all the little kiddies and tell them to join in on the fun. Who knows, it might be a real…*blast*. In the meantime, I'm going to take a short break and hand the spotlight back to my assistant, who will entertain you with a few jokes."

Clown stood up from the desk and vanished. A few seconds later, a second clown, who was obviously quite a bit larger, sat down with a joke book and began spouting out boring, mundane jokes that gave the viewing audience time to take a quick break.

Clown popped on a pair of night vision goggles, left the lavish office, and set a path toward Sarah's dressing room. If only the world knew the truth. If only the world knew that two people—and not an army of terrorists—were inside the studio holding five captive. If only the world knew that the two clowns inside were not as crazy as they were making themselves out to be. No, the two clowns were after justice—a justice the real world could never deliver. If only the world knew that a woman named Sophia Johnson and a man named Lyle Brickman were simply two scorned and very angry people who had decided it was time to destroy Sun Waves Studio for irreparable crimes that had been committed against them— well, against Sophia, at least. And if only the world knew Sophia and Lyle were being assisted by a very powerful man.

"The world will know," Sophia hissed under her clown mask as she made her way toward Sarah's dressing room. "In the meantime, the bombs will keep the world at bay…for now."

Sophia arrived at the dressing room door, pulled out her Glock from under her cloak, and prepared for action. "I'm going to open the door," she called out, using the voice-altering device that was attached to the mouth of the clown mask. "I want everyone lined up in a single line. If you refuse, I will detonate the bombs."

"Pete, hang tight…the clown is here. I'm going to leave my cell phone on and put it in my dress pocket." Sarah quickly dropped the cell phone down into the front pocket of her dress. "Okay, everyone, line up against the back wall— hurry."

Ryan, Patty, and Jill did as Sarah ordered. Amanda glanced at the dressing room door and then hurried to the back wall and placed herself beside Jill.

"We're in a line," Sarah called out and ran to Amanda.

Sophia eased the dressing room open, peered inside, and saw her five captives standing against the back wall. "Hands in the air!" she demanded. Sarah urged everyone to raise their hands into the air. "Very good," Sophia said in a pleased voice as she stepped through the doorway of the dressing room and studied her five captives. "The show is going to begin soon," she stated. "Of course, you all have your cell phones and have been watching my broadcast, no doubt."

"Who are you…why are you doing this?" Ryan yelled.

"Oh please, spare me the whining," Sophia snapped. She raised her left hand and pointed at Ryan while aiming the Glock directly at Patty. "One of you is a killer…and you will have exactly twenty-four hours to decide who. If you fail to produce the killer…you all die. If you produce the killer…you all live…and only the killer dies. It's that simple."

"Is it?" Sarah asked in a curious voice.

Sophia locked her eyes on Sarah. "I have three bombs set up," she explained, assuming each of her captives had their cell phones hidden and were recording her every word. Most likely Sarah, the smart-mouthed, arrogant cop, had advised the captives to keep their phones on. No matter, Sophia wanted her voice recorded and broadcast to the police. "Trip wires have been attached to each entry and exit door along with motion detection devices. There are also hidden cameras monitoring all the outside commotion. If anyone dares try to enter this studio I will blow us all up." Sophia switched her eyes to Jill, who was about ready to faint from fear. "I know this studio very well, Ms. Nayforth. I could, as they say, walk around this building blindfolded. You better tell Mr. Earton that, too."

"I haven't spoke—" Jill began to mutter.

"Don't lie to me, Ms. Nayforth," Sophia warned Jill. "You have all been allowed to keep your cell phones. I know you have spoken to Mr. Earton. You better warn him that if he wants to save his building, he better keep the cops back. After all, Mr. Earton cares more about his property than people, right?"

"Who are you!" Ryan demanded. "I demand you let us go."

"In time," Sophia promised. "In time you will either produce the killer or…die. It's that simple." Sophia narrowed her angry eyes. "If you give me the killer…you all live. If you fail…you all die. Those are the rules. When my view count reaches ten million, the game will begin."

"What sort of game?" Sarah asked.

"You will all be brought out onto the main stage and from there," Sophia explained in a harsh tone, "you will all be given games to play. If you fail to win the games, one of you will die…which means each game will require teamwork. If you win the game, you will be given one question, and each question will lead you to the killer—if you're smart, that is."

"My friend is pregnant," Amanda snapped at Sophia. "She is in no condition to play your stupid games…and if you hurt her…so help me I'll cook you into a pudding and feed you to the rats!"

"Calm down, Ms. Muffin," Sophia warned Amanda. "Our famous detective is going to be a coach of sorts. I'm not a monster…yet." Sophia turned to Sarah. "I want the killer, Detective. If you value your life and the life of your baby… play the game and be smart."

"We'll play your game," Sarah assured Sophia, staring into the darkness at the clown. All she could see was a dark shadow standing in the dressing room doorway. Sophia could clearly see Sarah staring at her. "You know there is no possible chance you'll escape," Sarah said.

"So it seems," Sophia informed Sarah. "If I don't get my

killer, we'll all never escape. If I get my killer…perhaps there might be a way for all of us to escape…except for one." Sophia let out a hideous laugh and then slammed the dressing room door closed.

Sarah immediately went for her cell phone. "Pete—"

"I heard every word," Pete promised Sarah as his sharp eyes studied the large studio. "Kiddo, no one out here is going to dare chance storming inside. Looks like we're going to have a very long wait ahead of us." Pete chewed on his cigar and looked at Conrad. "I'm giving the phone back to Conrad and going to talk to Detective Wallace."

Conrad took the cell phone back and rubbed his eyes. "It's a mess out here, Sarah. I feel like I'm trapped in a circus with a bunch of idiotic clowns."

"There are some good people left in Los Angeles," Sarah promised Conrad. "If I'm not mistaken, Roger Blake should be somewhere out there."

"Captain Blake transferred to Sacramento. Some young, smug guy named Hills took his place," Conrad informed Sarah as the sky overhead grew darker and darker. "Hills is in charge of the bomb squad…guy doesn't have a clue."

"You better warn him that there are trip wires, motion detectors, and hidden cameras," Sarah stated in an urgent voice. If Conrad said Hills was a nincompoop, Sarah believed him. "Don't let Hills try to do anything stupid."

"Try anything?" Conrad said. "The bomb squad is out here walking around without a clue. Hills hasn't stepped within fifty yards of the studio." Conrad shook his head in disgust. "A guy named Matt seems to have some brains to him. He told me that he advised Hills to stand clear of the studio for now. Detective Wallace is trying to set up a communication hotline to reach inside." Conrad glanced up at the darkening sky again. "Sarah…honey…I know there are good cops out here, but I doubt any cop I'm seeing is going to be able to save you. I—"

"I know, honey," Sarah whispered. "I know I have to act." Sarah glanced toward the dressing room door. "For now, I have to play the game. I have no other choice. I don't know how many…clowns…there are. I'm walking in the dark here. I need time."

"When the viewer count hits ten million, you'll have twenty-four hours. We all will," Conrad told Sarah in a miserable, worried voice. "Do you have your gun?"

"I have my backup," Sarah whispered. "I can get off a clean shot if needed—and it may come to that. Sarah checked the time on her cell phone. There was still plenty of daylight left. "What did Pete come up with concerning Leah Mayes?"

"He hasn't told me," Conrad said.

"I guess Pete was more interested in getting to the studio," Sarah replied, trying to hear Conrad over the sounds of cop cars and fire trucks. "Honey, if…something happens—"

"Nothing is going to happen. Do you hear me!" Conrad insisted, fighting back tears.

Sarah touched her tender tummy and whispered a sweet love to her unborn baby. "Yes…nothing is going to happen," she promised. "For now, all I can do is wait and play the game our angry clown has designed." Sarah touched her tummy again, closed her eyes, and began to pray.

Chapter Five

The lights on the main stage popped on like an explosion, nearly blinding Sarah and Amanda. Sarah quickly shielded her eyes with her arm and threw her eyes around. She spotted Sophia standing behind a wooden stand. Lyle was standing off to the side holding an assault rifle that could cut down a line of people within seconds; the rifle was a military M-16, and the way Lyle was holding it made Sarah wonder if the man had military training.

"Welcome," Sophia said in a pleasant voice and aimed a gray tablet at Sarah. "We're live, folks. Over ten million people —minus the boring cops—are viewing our program." Sophia quickly scanned Amanda, Jill, Patty, and Ryan. "Will all five contestants please sit down."

Sarah spotted five wooden chairs sitting in the middle of the stage, set in a circle formation; each chair had a set of handcuffs assigned to it. "Come on, June Bug," she whispered as she walked to the chairs and sat down facing the empty studio audience area. Amanda quickly sat down next to Sarah, forcing Jill, Patty, and Ryan to take seats that were not directly facing Sophia.

"Will each contestant please handcuff yourself to the person on your immediate left," Sophia ordered in a cheerful voice.

Sarah squinted and struggled to see past the stage. The stage lights were so bright it was impossible to see the studio audience viewing area. All Sarah could make out were vague shadows that looked like people. In reality, the shadows were nothing more than cardboard cut-outs of glaring clowns holding rifles, but because the lights were so bright, it was impossible to tell the difference—leaving Sarah and the cops to believe that more than two terrorists were present inside the studio.

Lyle wasn't too worried either way. A computer screen was sitting on a small table to his right. If anyone tried to enter the studio through any of the doors or windows, the motion detectors would signal an alarm. Lyle and Sophia would make tracks and escape into a hidden passage located under the backstage and then set off the bombs. The stage was located in the center of the studio, giving the two clowns a firm one-minute head start before any cop could reach their destination —plenty of time.

"Do as ordered," Sarah told everyone. She handcuffed her left wrist to Amanda and Ryan handcuffed his left wrist to Sarah's right wrist.

"Very good," Sophia announced and then set the tablet down onto a metal tripod that Lyle had rigged up. The tripod had wires hooked to it, allowing Lyle to move it back and forth by a remote control. "You're the cameraman," Sophia called out to Lyle. Lyle nodded, placed his rifle down against the table the computer screen was sitting on, and pulled a black remote control out of his pants pocket.

Sophia slowly approached the circle of chairs. "Ladies and gentlemen," she called out, speaking as if she were in the center ring of a major circus, "I present you with a game I call 'Find the Killer.' One of the five people you see sitting before your very eyes is a killer. But who? Oh, now, isn't that the question?"

Sarah looked up at the creepy clown mask Sophia was wearing and struggled to decide if the person was a man or a woman. The voice-altering device attached to the inside of the clown mask made it impossible to use the voice as an identifying factor. But as Sarah studied Sophia, she watched how the woman moved her arms and how she walked, studying the body language rather than the voice. *A woman,* Sarah confirmed in her mind. *This clown is a woman and the other clown is a man.*

"What do you want?" Jill cried out, handcuffed to Amanda and Patty. "Why did you ruin my show?"

"Contestant number five will remain silent," Sophia ordered and then pointed at the tablet. "Allow me to introduce our contestants," she stated in a fun voice. "Are you ready?"

Lyle glanced at the tablet and saw the viewer count climbing. He nodded at Sophia and waited.

Sophia grinned. She danced over to Sarah. "Contestant number one is Detective Sarah Garland!" she said in an excited voice and began clapping her gloved hands together. "Detective Garland is famous for catching both the Back Alley

Killer and the daughter of the Back Alley Killer. Can we all give her a big hand?"

All around the world people—mostly millennials who had no discipline and a hate for the law—began clapping their hands, sitting in dorky bedrooms, snotty coffee shops, arrogant dorm rooms, and other locations that sheltered diseased minds.

"Contestant number two," Sophia continued, "comes to us all the way from across the big pond. Can we all give it up for Amanda Hardcastle, our gal from London?"

"Kiss my muffins!" Amanda snapped at Sophia in a thick British accent.

Sophia titled her head back and laughed. "Oh, contestant number two, you are a riot," she laughed and then moved on. "Contestant number three is a makeup artist who can't even do her own nails. Give it up for Patty Darling...if that is her real name." Sophia moved around to Ryan. "Contestant number four is a pampered brat who wouldn't know a blister from a sideburn. Please welcome Ryan Mables!" Sophia patted Ryan's cheek with a hard hand and then moved on to Jill. "And last but not least, please welcome Jill Nayforth, who lives to brown-nose Earton!"

"Why are you doing this?" Jill cried. "What has Mr. Earton done that has caused you to ruin my show? I worked so hard!"

"Of course you have." Sophia laughed and danced back to the wooden stand like a little girl dancing down a candy store. "And now, let me introduce myself and my assistant," she exploded in an excited voice. "You may call me 'Clown' and you may call my assistant...yes, you guessed it...'Clown Two.'" Lyle picked up a voice box and pressed a button.

Cheesy laughter exploded into the air. "Thank you." Sophia took a bow and then pointed her right hand at Sarah.

"Now, ladies and gentlemen, allow me to explain the rules of the game. Detective Sarah Garland, because she is in a… delicate state…will be a coach. Her job will be to instruct the other four contestants on how to play each game I have designed. The other four contestants will work as a team to play…and win…the game. If they win, I will release a question that will give a clue as to who the killer is. If the contestants fail to win a game…they all die. Not a single game can be lost."

Lyle pressed a button on the voice box again and a roar of happy claps entered the air.

"Thank you…I love the rules, too. However, if the contestants somehow survive all of my games…with the help of Detective Garland…and receive all the clues…and identity the killer…all but the killer will be allowed to leave the studio alive." Lyle pressed a third button. An eruption of boos flooded the stage. "Yes, I know…but those are the rules, and it wouldn't be fair if I didn't play by the rules I have set."

Sarah studied Sophia with careful eyes. Jill, Patty, or Ryan was the killer Sophia was after. But why go through all the lights and action to pursue a killer inside of a studio building, involve the law, and mark yourself as a target? Sophia was out to make a statement in order to create a tidal wave of damage. The deranged clown Sarah was staring at wanted a powerful studio audience to watch certain events unfold in order to reveal a killer that was somehow connected to the studio—that Sarah was certain of, which made her thoughts return to Jill, Patty, and Ryan.

Patty and Ryan were engaged to be married. Ryan's

mother, Cecilia, obviously did not want her son marrying Patty. But what connection did that personal war have with the studio? Sarah wasn't certain, which made her think about Jill. Jill was a producer who had worked at the Sun Waves studio for many years. The woman had produced a few hit shows and two popular game shows but then had fallen into a slump due to her divorce. *Pregnant Bliss* had been created to help pull Jill back into the limelight. But was Jill a killer? Sarah wasn't certain.

"What is the first game?" she asked Sophia in a calm voice.

"In time," Sophia promised. "We have twenty-four hours to play only three games, Detective. We must not rush." Sophia reached down, picked up a stack of papers sitting on the wooden stand, and cleared her throat. "First we're going to get to know each other a little better. I want my viewing audience to really know who my five contestants are." Lyle pressed the sound box. Applause and cheers thundered into the air. "Thank you…thank you," Sophia said. She took a bow and then got down to business. "I hold in my hands personal information that I'm afraid…" Sophia lifted her left hand over the lips of her creepy clown mask and made an *oops* motion, "is very sensitive information my contestants may object to being made…shall we say…public?"

Patty glanced over at Ryan. Ryan's face suddenly twisted into an expression of terror. Sweat began pouring down the sides of his head. "Does she know?" she whispered.

"How should I know?" Ryan whispered back in a sharp tone.

"No, no," Sophia warned, hearing Patty and Ryan whispering back and forth. "I will not allow you to be rude to my viewing audience." Sophia quickly picked up her Glock, left the wooden post, and walked directly to Patty. "If I hear any more whispering," she threatened and then aimed the gun at Patty, "we will be short one contestant. Is that clear?"

"Yeah…please don't hurt her," Ryan pleaded. "No more whispering…I promise."

"Very good," Sophia hissed. She lowered the gun and then slapped Ryan across his face with her left hand. "I mean business, get it?" she told him in a voice that worried Sarah. Whoever the clown was—whoever the woman beneath the clown mask was—she was no stranger to violence.

"I get it…I get it," Ryan whimpered.

"You better," Sophia warned and then returned to the wooden post. "I apologize to my viewing audience for the interruption, but I'm afraid there comes a time when I must be…more stern than I prefer to be." Sophia put away her gun, grabbed the stack of papers, and cleared her voice. "Now, where were we?" she said, forcing her voice to sound cheerful. "Oh yes…sensitive information." Lyle let three loud sounds of applause into the air again. "We are going to begin with Detective Garland." Applause and cheers erupted. Sophia locked her eyes on Sarah. "Detective, it has been brought to my attention that you were once divorced and now are remarried to a cop from New York. Is that true?"

"Yes." Sarah nodded. Sophia grinned. "Is it also true that you and your new husband rob banks together across the state of Alaska?"

"What?" Amanda gasped as her cheeks filled with anger. "Listen, you blimey piece of rotten—"

"Your turn will come, London," Sophia promised in a stern tone. "One more outburst and Patty Darling eats a bullet."

"It's all right," Sarah promised Amanda. She focused on Sophia with careful eyes. Sophia was playing a game. "Yes, it's true."

"What?" Amanda nearly wet her pants. "Sarah—"

Sarah quickly gave Amanda a *play along* eye. Amanda didn't know what to think. All she wanted to do was punch Sophia square in the face. "Uh…sorry…no more outbursts."

"See to it," Sophia warned, confused as to why Sarah had admitted to a lie. "So you admit that you and your new husband rob banks?"

"Yes," Sarah said. "We also rob donut shops, candy shops, and hardware stores. We're working our way up to book shops." Sarah's intention was to make Sophia appear foolish and to discredit her authority. "Someday we plan to rob a cake shop and sell all the stolen goods to a group of children we know in Iowa."

Sophia frowned. Sarah had made her appear foolish, which meant the questions she had written up to attack the character of each contestant would be clownish instead of damaging. "Might I remind you, Detective, that I require honest answers," she hissed. She dropped the stack of papers and went for the Glock 17. "Any more games and your little British friend dies."

"So kill her," Sarah told Sophia in a calm voice.

"What?" Amanda gasped. "Uh…love—"

"It's okay," Sarah promised. While Sophia was no stranger to violence, the woman certainly wasn't going to kill an innocent person in front of millions. Sophia wasn't going to risk becoming a villain in the eyes of the people she was working so desperately to manipulate. If the woman dared carry out a vile murder without cause, the viewing audience would certainly turn against her. "She isn't going to harm anyone…not yet…not until the games are played. Isn't that right?"

Sophia glared at Sarah with eyes dripping with lava. The cop was smart—too smart. "You're right, Detective," she told Sarah, deciding to use the woman's game against her. "Unlike one of you, I'm not a killer." Sophia put her gun away. "I'll move on to London," she stated in a quick voice and then added: "I would answer my questions honestly, London, or your friend will be taken away and stuffed into a dark closet."

"Oh, just ask your silly questions," Amanda snapped. "I'm hungry. I want some Chick-Fil-A and Krispy Kreme donuts and a long nap…so stop wasting my time and get on with it."

A twenty-year-old British man vacationing in Los Angeles with a group of friends held out his hand. "Pay up," he told a skinny brown-haired man. "I told you she would be sassy." The brown-haired man sighed and pulled a twenty-dollar bill out of his wallet. Although Amanda might appear weak and timid, she had a brave mouth.

Sophia didn't appreciate Amanda's smart mouth, but time was running out, and she didn't have time to put Amanda in her place. Besides, she wasn't even interested in Amanda— Amanda was simply extra baggage attached to Sarah, an extra prop. The questions Sophia had written up in the fancy office concerning Sarah and Amanda were meant to weaken them in the eyes of the viewing audience. The real questions, the juicy ones, pertaining to Jill, Patty, and Ryan…well, those questions had been created and stored away in a safe place over a month ago. Sophia wasn't even aware when she and Lyle began to create their plan of revenge that Sarah and Amanda would even be part of the show. After finding out that Sarah was going to be the very first contestant, Sophia had decided to use the cop as a bottle of honey to pour on some bread in order to attack the ants—and to help draw out a killer while throwing pie in the woman's face. Of course, the questions she had created to act as pie to throw at Sarah didn't exactly work out as planned.

Chapter Six

"London, my source has revealed to me that you are a shoplifter. Is that true?" Sophia asked Amanda in a stern tone. "Might I remind you…answer the way I expect, or your friend will vanish." Sophia narrowed her eyes and studied Sarah. Yes, Sarah had thrown pie back in her face, but now it was time to dismantle Amanda's credibility and use threats to achieve the task.

Amanda glanced at Sarah. Sarah was staring at the deranged clown with careful eyes. "Oh…" Amanda winced. She couldn't risk Sarah being harmed. The stupid clown had lost its battle against Sarah but had pressed Amanda into a corner. "I…yes…I shoplift," she lied in order to please Sophia.

"And isn't it true that your dear friend and her new husband rob banks?" Sophia demanded, determined to win over Sarah. "Answer the right way," she warned.

"It's true," Sarah spoke for Amanda in a tone that pleased Sophia.

"Very good." Sophia clapped her hands. "So we have a crooked cop and a thief on our show."

Lyle hit the sound box. Applause erupted into the brightly lit air. Sophia wasn't certain if her viewing audience had bought the cookie; she was sure the skunk cops hovering around outside hadn't, but that was okay. What mattered was that she had won the battle...and that's all that ever mattered to Sophia: destroying people who dared become her enemy.

"Now, let's move on to Jill Nayforth," Sophia said, pretending to sound excited. "Jill, isn't it true that you are Mr. Earton's daughter?"

Jill's face froze. Her eyes became wide and white, filled with shock and fear. "I...how did you...I mean...no...no... you're lying!" she said, starting off in a whispering whimper and ending up in a frantic scream.

"You mean it's not true that you blackmailed Mr. Earton into giving you a job at Sun Waves Studio?" Sophia asked Jill and then held up what looked like an authentic birth certificate. "Is this not your birth certificate, Jill?" she asked. "And is this not the signature of one Mr. Earton in the spot marked 'Father'?" Sophia danced over to the tablet and showed the viewing audience the birth certificate, grinned, and then danced back to the wooden post. "Jill, Jill, shame on you for lying to my viewing audience."

"You're...it's all a lie!" Jill cried.

"So are you," Sophia laughed and then moved on to Patty. "Patty...darling..." she teased, "does the name Richie Stewart ring a bell?"

Patty, like Jill, froze up for a few seconds.

"Who?" Ryan asked.

"Who is the question." Sophia beamed. "Patty, why don't you tell your fiancé who Richie Stewart is?"

"I…don't know who the guy is," Patty lied. "Never heard of that name before…you're barking up the wrong tree."

"Am I?" Sophia asked and quickly presented a photo to her viewing audience. The photo was of a young man who appeared to be a tough biker-type character. "Is this not your secret boyfriend?"

"What?" Ryan yelled in shock, staring at the photo. And then something horrible happened: The face in the photo clicked in his troubled mind. "Hey, I recognize that guy…he's the mechanic who worked on my Jeep!" Ryan swung his head around at Patty. "You've…been…cheating on me?"

"No…" Patty's cheeks turned red. "It's all a lie," she spat at Sophia. "Richie…he's…"

"Who?" Sophia asked in a happy voice. "Patty, do tell my viewing audience who Richie Stewart is." Sophia danced over to the tablet again and gave her viewing audience a closer look at the young man in question. "And might I remind my viewing audience that Patty was the last person to have worked on poor Leah Mayes before the woman…shall we say…kicked the bucket?"

"Who is this guy, Patty?" Ryan demanded.

Sophia grinned and returned to her post. Dividing the contestants before the games began was working out deliciously. Sure, Sarah had been a wart and she had to twist Amanda's arm, but so what? Jill, Patty, and Ryan would add a cherry to the flat pie. And, Sophia reminded herself, those viewing the show probably didn't have enough brain cells left to form a single objective thought. The world wanted entertainment—not facts. "Yes, Patty, do tell us who Richie Stewart is."

"I…can't," Patty answered in a miserable voice.

Sophia nodded at Lyle. Lyle hit the sound box. Boos filled the air. "Oh well, I guess we will move on to Ryan Mables," she announced, pretending to sound disappointed. "Ryan, is it true that your mother, Cecilia Mables, murdered your dad?"

"What?" Ryan said in a shocked voice. "What kind of crazy question is that?" he demanded. "My mother never harmed my dad—"

"But your dad is dead?"

"Yeah…but my parents divorced two years before he died," Ryan insisted. "My dad died in a car accident. We weren't even close."

"But isn't it true that your mother inherited your dad's money after he died?" Sophia pressed.

"I…my mother was already receiving alimony payments… large amounts," Ryan confessed. "I was fifteen years old at the time."

"And your dad died two years later, just as you were preparing to turn into an adult. Curious," Sophia said, throwing suspicion into the air. "Curious how your mother never remarried, either."

"My mother is a very busy woman," Ryan snapped at Sophia. "I…" Ryan threw his eyes down at the stage floor and went silent.

"So we have a crooked cop, a thief, a liar, a dishonest fiancé, and the son of a killer. Let's give a big hand for our five contestants," Sophia shouted and began clapping her hands.

"No one is buying this," Conrad growled in an angry voice, staring at a television sitting in the womb of a gray police van.

"Oh yeah?" a skinny cop named Steve said. "Look at the comments…this guy from New York is running all five of our hostages into the mud…and this girl from Wisconsin is claiming she is going to call the FBI and have them investigate you and your wife for bank robbery."

Conrad glanced away from the television that was sitting on a metal rack and studied a computer screen. Steve was on Sophia's social media page. Thousands of comments were pouring in…the majority of the comments were extremely negative toward Sarah, Amanda, Jill, Patty, and Ryan; and, not surprisingly, the comments that were focused on Sophia and Lyle—even though nobody in the world was aware of who the two clowns who had appeared to the viewing audience were— were extremely positive. Comments such as "Clowns Rock" and "My new favorite show" and "Give it to 'em clown" were very popular. Comments such as "Hang 'em," "Feed 'em poison pie," and "Drown the liars" were popular against the innocent; at least Sarah and Amanda.

Conrad glanced over at Pete. Pete was chewing on a half-smoked cigar wearing a scowl on his face. "The world is rotten," Pete said in a disgusted voice. "Back in my day we would have hunted down rats making comments like those."

"Social media is a disease," Conrad agreed as sweat poured down his face. The inside of the van felt like a sweat factory. "Any news on Leah Mayes?"

"Basic fluff," Pete explained, ignoring the heat. The inside of a sweltering police van was home to him. "Born and raised in Los Angeles…became a model after high school…got married…divorced two weeks later…played the night life scene…got arrested once for being caught with a small amount of cocaine…ended up landing a gig hosting this new game show. I couldn't find anything damaging or worrisome."

"Random target?" Conrad asked.

"Seems that way," Pete said, nodding. "Our clown person is making the clowns watching her think Leah Mayes is the victim she wants someone to confess to murdering…at least that's the way I see it. But who knows…there could be more to Leah Mayes than we understand." Pete rubbed his chin. "We don't have a lot to go on right now."

"Can't we track the social media page the clowns are using?" Conrad asked and pointed at the computer screen Steve was staring at. "Steve?"

"The page was created last year and left unused until now," Steve explained. "Millions of dummy pages are created every day…there's no way to track them." Steve turned in a gray chair, wiped sweat off his forehead, and looked up at Conrad. "The name and email address used to create the page are linked to a spam email that was created in Russia."

Conrad shoved his hands into the pockets of his leather jacket. "Yeah…" he said in a frustrated voice. "We're walking blind, right? I mean, these clowns just walked into that studio in broad daylight, set up three bombs, killed a woman, and then took my wife hostage without anyone seeing, right?"

"Detective Spencer," Steve began. Steve was usually on desk duty and rarely even wore a gun.

"What?" Conrad barked. "What are you going to say? The Los Angeles Police Department is doing its best? Is that it?"

Pete grabbed Conrad's arm and pulled him out of the van. "Cool it," he ordered in a tough voice. "That kid isn't responsible for this mess. But I know who is."

Conrad studied Pete's stern face. "Mr. Earton."

"Yep." Peter nodded. "I can't get a word with the guy." Pete turned away from the police van and studied a long row of studios, some appearing like airport hangars while others resembled tall apartment buildings. "You're right, Conrad… those clowns didn't walk in here in broad daylight. Someone has been letting them in. The question is, who?"

"Maybe we need to find Mr. Earton and find out," Conrad stated in a determined voice.

"Conrad, this is Los Angeles," Pete explained as he chewed on his cigar. "If Mr. Earton doesn't want to talk to the police, the man won't talk to the police. You have to understand that you're looking at millions and millions of dollars that involve some pretty powerful people…including the IRS. Mr. Earton may be the owner of Sun Waves Studio, but his hands are tied to other people—other people he's probably in meetings with right this second."

"Look, Pete, I'm a New York cop," Conrad pointed out as cops, firefighters, and bomb squad personnel roamed around like lost puppies. "I get the layout, okay. I'm not a small-town hick cop who handles school crossings."

"Then you should know what I'm thinking," Pete told Conrad and then offered a clever grin.

"Security cameras."

"Mr. Earton is a powerful man and right now, I doubt there is a judge in Los Angeles who will issue a legal search warrant. But," Pete tossed a thumb back at the cop van, "that young kid inside that van seems to have some brains."

"Let's go find out," Conrad said in a hurried voice. Pete quickly grabbed his arm. "What?"

"Listen," Pete told Conrad in a careful voice, "let me talk to the kid, okay? You're an outsider and I'm not. My name still carries some weight."

Conrad knew Pete made a good point. "You're a good cop, Pete…one of the best, in my opinion. Sorry for being—"

"Don't apologize," Pete scolded Conrad and then patted the man's shoulder. "Spencer, in the short time I've known you I've come to understand what Sarah sees in you. You're a good man and a good cop, but at the end of the day we're also human. Your pregnant wife is trapped inside that studio with some psychos wearing clown masks…and that's enough to make any decent husband lose his cool."

Conrad glanced up at the towering studio Sarah was trapped in. "Pete, if anything happens to Sarah…I mean…I almost lost her once when she and Amanda went to that remote hot springs location…I can't lose her." Conrad's eyes filled with worry and sorrow. "I tell Sarah that I…love her, you know?" Pete nodded. "But Pete, you know…that woman is… she's the reason I get out of bed each morning. And now that we're going to have a baby, my entire world has changed." Pete nodded again, patiently listening to Conrad. "I have a family now…you, Amanda, Manford…you're all my family, too… and I don't want to lose that." Conrad looked up at the studio again. "Sarah is a smart cop…" he tried to comfort his worried heart.

"Yes, she is…and so are we," Pete assured Conrad. "The lights went out in that studio…bombs were set…a woman was killed…and now the lights are back on. Conrad, all of that didn't happen overnight." Pete tossed a thumb at the studio. "The bomb-sniffing dogs have sniffed out this place and let us know that three exit doors on the north side are scented with bombs. These clowns have been at this for a while." Pete chewed on his cigar. "I know a few tidbits about Mr. Earton, but not enough…but what I do know about the man never set well in my gut. The studios are dark and crooked places, Conrad." Pete patted Conrad's shoulder again and made his way back inside the cop van. "What do we have?" he asked Steve.

"A bunch of talking," Steve answered Pete and quickly searched for Conrad. "Where is—"

"Taking a walk," Pete explained and then placed a heavy hand down onto Steve's shoulder. "Son," he said in a serious voice, "just how smart are you?"

Steve raised his skinny face up at Pete. "I was beat up a lot in high school and the girls ignored me…everyone called me 'Screech.' Why? Because I was smart," Steve told Pete in a proud voice. "I may not be someone who has a thousand girls at his side, but I am someone who can outsmart any piece of technology there is around—and I'm guessing that's what you want, right?"

Pete grinned. "I knew your dad, son. He was a good cop. I figure you became a cop because—"

"After my dad was killed in the line of duty, I ditched the Air Force." Steve nodded. "I may not be on the SWAT team, but I'm sure Dad is proud of me."

"I know he is," Pete agreed and carefully sat down next to Steve. "Okay, son, I need a whole bunch of security—"

"Say no more," Steve quickly cut Pete off. "I'll backdate thirty days."

"How soon?"

"Give me two or three hours," Steve answered and then looked at Pete with proud eyes. "A good cop knows something fishy is going on."

"And you're a good cop," Pete assured Steve and then climbed back out into the sun and studied the studio building. The dark clouds that had formed earlier but faded off were quickly returning. A storm was certainly forming.

Chapter Seven

"We'll be back after a quick ten-minute break," Sophia spoke into the tablet. "In the meantime, go get a snack, use the bathroom, and hurry back…because the first game is about to begin." Sophia nodded at Lyle. Lyle quickly stepped up to the tablet, turned it away from the stage, and began telling mundane jokes again. "In the meantime," Sophia hissed, marching over to Sarah and getting in her face, "no more playing smart cop, do you hear me!"

Sarah kept her eyes low. "I'm a cop," she informed Sophia. "What do you expect from me? You asked a stupid question and I made you look foolish. That's how the game works."

Sophia threw out her right hand and grabbed Sarah's chin. "I'm in charge, is that clear?" she snapped in a dangerous tone. "If you want to live, you better play by my rules."

"Asking a stupid question isn't smart," Sarah told Sophia, standing her ground. "Your goal was to cast doubt on my character. Why? Because you want your viewing audience standing in your corner. You know the cops aren't buying your lies…but the viewing audience, if you can muster them into a supportive army…" Sarah stopped talking in order to give Sophia room to think.

"Who is Richie Stewart?" Ryan demanded, stepping on Sarah's toes. "How did you get a photo of that guy? Tell me!"

Sophia scowled at Sarah and then released her chin and looked at Ryan. "Why don't you ask your little fiancé?"

"You're going to pay big time for this," Patty threatened Sophia. "I don't know who you are…who is wearing that stupid mask…but you're going to pay big time."

"Am I?" Sophia challenged Patty. "All I want is the killer."

"You killed Leah Mayes," Sarah told Sophia. "Leah Mayes was part of this scheme, right? Maybe—maybe she knew too much? Maybe she was in the way? Who knows? But you did kill her."

Sophia stared at Patty's angry face for a few seconds and then turned back to Sarah. "So what if I did? I'm after another killer, Detective," she stated, forcing calmness to her voice. "I'm after—"

"You're after a killer…but the people behind the scenes are after a lot more, right?" Sarah asked Sophia in a careful voice.

"You're not as stupid as I had hoped you would be," Sophia answered Sarah.

"What are you talking about?" Jill demanded, unable to see Sarah or Sophia. "Please, I want answers…how did you find out that Mr. Earton is my biological father?"

"Maybe *she* didn't find out on *her* own," Sarah told Jill. "Maybe someone more powerful gave her the information."

Lyle stopped telling his mundane jokes and looked at Sarah. Sarah was catching on far too fast—and becoming a grave danger. Sophia shook her head at Lyle and ordered him to continue entertaining the viewing audience. "It doesn't matter what you think is…or isn't, Detective," she said. "I want one killer…either I get the killer or you all die. It's that simple. As far as the rest of the game goes…there may be other players, but that is of no concern to you." Sophia folded her arms. "My responsibility is to play the first quarter of the game and put the home team in a winning position. But rest assured…I do have my personal reasons for standing here, and I will have my killer." Sophia stared at Sarah with sour eyes. "And yes…I am a woman," she confessed. "This is a woman's game show, after all, right?"

"I'd like to slug you," Amanda told Sophia and raised her right hand and formed a fist. "When this is all over, I'm going to slug you right in the nose…POW!"

"Dream on." Sophia rolled her eyes. "You're of no concern to me. The only reason you're here, London, is because you shadow your friend. The detective is the real star. You're just a bothersome gnat I had to include."

"I wouldn't make Amanda mad," Sarah warned Sophia. "I've seen this woman get mad…I would rather tangle with a wild bear."

"I'm scared," Sophia told Sarah in a sarcastic voice. "How much more time?"

"Three minutes," Lyle called out.

"Any problems?" Sophia asked.

"Motion sensors are silent," Lyle assured Sophia. "Our outside team is doing their job."

"Good." Sophia nodded and took her eyes to Sarah. "See that game over there?" she said and pointed to the "Diaper Rash" game that had been brought out earlier. Sarah nodded. "Your job will be to help your team find the correct diaper.

The correct diaper has a clue in it. If they open even one wrong diaper…guess what happens?"

"We get poop in our face?" Amanda asked in a rude voice.

"No…you get powdered poison in your face…the same kind of poison that killed Leah Mayes," Sophia promised. "The poison is laced with a mild acid that the victim can't feel at first. Once the acid burns into the skin…and by then, as Leah proved, the victim will feel the effect…the poison is released into the bloodstream and goes straight to the heart. Very deadly…very clever."

"You're crazy!" Patty screamed. "You're…insane!"

"I have rules to play by…but rest assured," Sophia assured Patty, "whether you survive all three games or die playing the first…the killer I'm after will suffer."

"You have rules to play by," Sarah spoke up, "which means you didn't set the rules, did you? No, the people behind the scenes set the rules, didn't they?"

"It's like I said, Detective," Sophia pointed out, "my job is to make sure the home team wins."

Lyle raised a finger into the air. "One minute."

Sophia walked back to the wooden post and prepared to return her attention back to the viewing audience. When Lyle shot a thumbs-up into the air, the woman cleared her throat and waved at the tablet.

"Welcome back," Sophia announced in a pleased voice. "I hope you grabbed a snack and used the bathroom because the first game is about to begin." Sophia pointed to the Diaper Rash game. Lyle used a remote control to turn the tablet in order to allow the viewing audience to see the game. "Our first game is called 'Poisonous Diaper,'" Sophia told her viewing audience in a daring voice. "All five contestants, with the help of their coach, will have one hour to locate the only diaper that isn't filled with poison. But here's the fun part…" Sophia paused, danced over to the Diaper Rash game, and began tapping each diaper with a gentle finger. "Once the contestants choose a diaper…only one of them will be chosen to open it…and that person will live…or die!" Lyle hit the voice box. Applause and cheers struck the stage.

"Let's hope the wrong diaper is chosen," Sophia teased and then laughed. "Now, on with the game." Sophia walked over to Sarah. "Detective Garland, you are the official coach. Your duty is to help the contestants locate the right diaper by guiding your team through a series of riddles."

"Riddles?" Sarah asked.

Sophia nodded. "I will ask each contestant a riddle…and you will be allowed to offer only one word that can assist them. If the riddle is not answered correctly, the contestant will be forced to go to the board and choose a diaper at random…and hope for the best. If the contestant answers the riddle correctly, I will give you a clue." Sophia clapped her hands together. "London, you're up!" she called out. She skipped back to the wooden post and picked up a piece of paper that had a series of riddles written on it. "Are you ready to play?"

Amanda glanced at Sarah. "Love, I stink at answering riddles…I'm talking rotten eggs, here." She gulped.

Sarah drew in an uneasy breath. "We can do this," she assured Amanda, staring at the Diaper Rash game. "Stay calm and think. You're a smart woman…a brilliant woman."

Amanda locked her eyes on the diapers attached to the game board and sighed. "I'm a dead woman," she uttered in a miserable voice.

Sophia grinned. Seeing Sarah and Amanda sweat a little was great! "Okay, London, here is your riddle. Coach, are you ready?" Sarah reluctantly nodded yes. "London," Sophia continued, "what has a long lifespan but has not begun to live?" She pointed a hard finger at Amanda. "Remember, Coach, you get only one word. The clock is ticking. You have five minutes."

The riddles, at least to Sophia, because she had created the riddles herself, were clever and ingenious. However, Sarah immediately knew the answer, surprised that the riddle was so simple. She turned her head and looked at Amanda. "My one word," she announced in a clear, loud voice, "to assist you is: baby."

Amanda stared into Sarah's eyes and then felt a wave of relief tear through her troubled heart. "Oh…of course…the answer to the riddle is a baby. A baby that isn't born could live to be a hundred…but the baby isn't born yet."

Sophia frowned. "You have answered the riddle… correctly," she said in a disappointed, angry voice. Lyle glanced down at his computer screen and saw numerous comments appear—comments that attacked the riddle, marking it as "Lame" and "Stupid." Lyle wanted to tell Sophia that the riddles she had created weren't difficult to figure out, but because he was in love with the woman, and understood the real objective of the game, Lyle knew the riddles weren't important enough to upset Sophia over.

"My clue, please," Sarah told Sophia. "Your viewing audience is watching. Play by the rules you set."

Sophia scowled at Sarah with bitter eyes. Oh, how she wanted to throw a diaper full of poison in the woman's face. Instead, she surrendered the first clue. "Of course," she stated, struggling to appear calm in front of her viewing audience. "The first clue is a math question. What is the square root of nine hundred…minus the months a woman is pregnant?"

Sarah ran some numbers through her mind. But it was Amanda who spoke first. "Are we talking about an average pregnancy?" she asked Sophia in a thoughtful voice. "A pregnancy can differ by days or even weeks."

"Yes, yes, an average pregnancy," Sophia snapped at Amanda in an annoyed tone.

"No need to get snippy, you snot," Amanda snapped. "I simply asked a question." Amanda rolled her eyes. "The answer is twenty-one, love."

Sarah nodded and studied the diapers. They were numbered 1-20. There was no number 21. "Okay, next riddle," she ordered Sophia.

Sophia glared at Sarah with eyes that could have burst into flames. "Patty Darling, you're up!" she announced. "Are you ready?"

Patty felt her stomach tighten. "Maybe Richie can help you, huh?" Ryan blasted Patty in a hateful voice. "My mother was right about you all along."

"No, she wasn't, Ryan," Patty pleaded. "I…Richie is…" Patty closed her eyes. "Oh, ask the stupid riddle!" she yelled as anger overwhelmed her sorrow.

Sophia didn't appreciate Patty's rudeness or tone but decided to play it cool. "Patty," she said, showing a stern tone, "what gives life to something that has been born? You have five minutes!" Sophia threw a hard eye at Sarah. "Remember, Coach, you—"

"Get one word. I know," Sarah assured Sophia as her mind

latched onto the answer. "Patty, honey?" she said, speaking in a soothing tone.

"What?" Patty snapped.

"Let me help you," Sarah told Patty, remaining calm and soothing. "Are you ready for the one word I'm allowed to give?"

Patty closed her eyes. "What was the stupid riddle again?" Sarah repeated it. "Okay…okay…I got it…what's your word?"

"Cow," Sarah stated in a clear voice. Sophia felt her left hand form into a deadly fist. Oh, how she hated—loathed— Sarah…but the orders were to play it nice with the pregnant cop.

Patty kept her eyes closed and began to think. "What gives life to something that has been born…cow?" Patty's eyes flung open. "Milk!" she hollered. "The answer is milk!"

"You are correct," Sophia said in a bitter voice as millions of viewers began throwing harsh reviews at her. Lyle shook his head but didn't say a word. Yeah, the riddles were dumb, but Sophia had insisted that each riddle was doused with a thick coat of brilliance. Lyle knew Sophia's pride and arrogance were the woman's downfall, but love kept the truth from being spoken. "Here is your next clue." Sarah glanced over at Amanda. Amanda nodded. "What is two hundred eighty-eight divided by twelve minus the answer to the last clue?"

"The answer is three," Amanda whispered to Sarah.

"You're good," Sarah complimented Amanda and studied diaper number three on the Diaper Rash game board. At the rate Sophia was going, locating the correct diaper was going to be a cinch…or was it? She still had Ryan and Jill to assist. What if Ryan or Jill was unable to answer a riddle?

"Ryan Mables, you're next," Sophia announced, becoming extremely bitter. "Are you ready?"

"I guess," Ryan declared. He shot Patty a sour eye and then turned his head away from her. "Go ahead and ask your silly riddle, lady. It doesn't matter…I've been betrayed…so what if I die? Who cares."

Sophia frowned. The attitude of her hostages was becoming very upsetting. Sophia demanded control and fear, and each of her hostages was showing her the opposite side of the coin. But, she thought, reminding herself that a very powerful man was watching, the show had to go on. "Ryan, what connects life but has to be severed in order for life to start?" Surely, Sophia thought, the riddle she threw at Ryan would offer some complication to the game.

"How should I know?" Ryan barked, struggling to hold his broken heart steady enough to speak. "Who cares!"

"Ryan," Sarah ordered in a stern voice, "answer the riddle, do you hear me?"

"Or what? Are you going to arrest me…or maybe you can arrest Patty's little boyfriend, huh?" Ryan snapped.

"Richie isn't my boyfriend," Patty declared in an angry but hurt voice. "Ryan, you don't understand…"

"I'm sure I do," Ryan fired back. "My mother was right. You're nothing but a gold digger. I should have known!" Ryan shook his head in disgust. "If I live through this, I'm going to marry the woman Mother has always wanted me to marry."

"Ryan, focus on the riddle and—" Sarah tried to speak.

"Oh shut up," Ryan yelled.

Sophia grinned. Maybe Ryan was going to make the show come alive after all.

Chapter Eight

Ryan jerked at his wrists, causing Sarah and Patty pain from the handcuffs. "Knock it off," Patty griped.

"Oh sure, blame me for this," Ryan griped back. "It's not my fault these handcuffs are cutting into my wrists."

Sarah forced patience to her mind. "Ryan, you need to focus," she ordered. "We have less than five minutes."

"Tick-tock," Sophia taunted Ryan.

Ryan rolled his eyes. Who cared about a stupid riddle? Patty had ripped his heart out and stomped all over it. Life was over. "I'll do this for Mother," he stated in a bitter voice. "Now…what is the riddle again?"

Sarah repeated it. "And my one word is: Cord."

Ryan rolled his eyes again in a sarcastic way that upset Sophia. "Well, duh, the answer is an umbilical cord. Any moron can guess that."

Lyle flinched. Sophia wouldn't appreciate being called a moron. He threw his eyes at the woman and watched her left hand begin to twitch. Not good. "What's the clue?" Sarah asked.

"Take your last answer and multiply it by two hundred forty-six…and then subtract the address of Richie," Sophia told Sarah through gritted teeth. "Only Patty Darling knows the address."

Ryan shot his head at Patty. "You do?"

Patty let out a miserable moan. "It's not what you think, Ryan."

"What's the address!" Ryan yelled at Patty. "I'll kill him!"

"No…please…" Patty struggled to turn around and see Sophia. "You stupid clown…you're going to pay!" she threatened Sophia. "All of you are!"

"What's the stupid address!" Ryan insisted.

"No way…" Patty shook her head. "I'm not going to put Richie's life in danger."

"Oh…so you would rather have me die instead?" Ryan snapped. "You make me sick!" Ryan turned his head away from Patty.

"Patty," Sarah spoke in a voice that told Patty she meant business, "we need the address…right now."

"Drop dead, cop," Patty fired at Sarah.

"Oh good grief," Amanda exploded. "Listen to me, you stupid little muffin, I don't care about your love life, but I do care about living, so you better shake the crumbs out of your brain before I sock you in the nose!"

"Give us the address," Jill ordered Patty in a pleading voice.

"Oh, if Patty Darling refuses to give the address," Sophia stated, feeling a grin replace her anger, "then she will be the first one to choose a diaper at random." Perhaps the riddles

Sophia created weren't working out as planned, but oh, the drama…spectacular entertainment.

Ryan snapped his head back around. "Patty, for the love of everything good, just give up the stupid address! There's no sense in dying."

Patty felt closed in and trapped. If she confessed Richie's address, every cop in the world would close in on his home. Richie was a man who was hiding in America…a man wanted by the police in Italy for running guns. Richie was also Patty's brother. There was only one thing to do. "Richie," Patty yelled, "don't go home…run to the hideout spot and stay there…I have to give your address…I'm sorry…just run!"

Richie Stewart, who was watching the show from the garage he worked at, glanced around at two other greasy mechanics who were hard at work, and then slipped away without being seen.

"Very noble," Sophia told Patty, "but it doesn't matter, does it? I'm sure the cops will track him down."

"You rat!" Patty screamed. "What did Richie ever do to you?"

"Shut up and give us the address," Ryan demanded.

Patty gritted her teeth. "720 East Shore Lane, Apartment…12B."

Amanda quickly did the math. "The answer is eighteen, love," she told Sarah.

Sarah nodded. "Next riddle."

Sophia hesitated. Surely Sarah and her math friend were going to guess the right diaper. If only the rules could be broken. The truth was, Sophia feared the man who was standing behind the scenes pulling all the strings. At the moment it was better to play by the rules, even if it meant allowing Sarah victory.

"Jill, are you ready?" she called out. Jill reluctantly nodded. "Jill, what is smooth as silk but turns into a prune?" Lyle shook his head. The riddles were so lame. Underneath the clown's mask was a beautiful woman who had captured Lyle's heart—a woman who was daring, mysterious, captivating, and intelligent…but a woman who stunk at writing riddles. Again, Lyle was quickly reminded of the arrogant pride that poisoned Sophia's heart; a pride that worried him.

"My word to you, Jill, is: butt."

Jill felt relief wash over her like a tidal wave as a very simple answer entered her mind. "The answer to the riddle is a baby's butt."

"You are…correct," Sophia told Jill and then simply rolled her eyes. "Jill, your clue is this. Take the last answer, divide it by two, and then multiply it by two…and then subtract today's date."

Amanda ran the math. "The answer is four."

Sophia glanced at the diapers hanging on the Diaper Rash game. Diaper number four glared back at her as if it were mocking her imbecilic game. She raised an angry finger and ordered Lyle to release Jill. "You are about to find out if the answer is correct," she stated, deciding to torment Jill.

Lyle left his station, freed Jill, and then walked her over to the Diaper Rash game.

"Please…" Jill begged.

"Open the diaper," Lyle ordered Jill in a deadly tone. He whipped out a Glock 19 and pressed the gun into the small of Jill's back. "Play the game, lady."

"I…" Tears began to fall from Jill's terrified eyes.

"No," Patty begged. "You monster…leave him alone!"

"Don't make me slap you again," Sophia warned.

"Take my handcuffs off me and I'll teach you to slap that girl," Amanda fired at Sophia. "You slapped a person who couldn't defend herself…I'll remember that."

"I'm shaking," Sophia snarled at Amanda and then focused back on Ryan. "Four minutes," she stated and then danced over to the Diaper Rash game and pulled diaper number 16 free. "Patty Darling, a present for you," she laughed.

"You monster!" Patty screamed. "Why don't you take off that stupid mask and show yourself!"

"Oh, and spoil the fun?" Sophia asked, walking the diaper over to Patty. "Not yet," she said, placing the diaper down on Patty's lap and then grabbing Ryan's face. "Three minutes."

Ryan felt panic enter his heart. If he confessed his secret, the cops would surely arrest him…and his mother would never forgive him. But it was either jail or see Patty die a horrifying death. "Okay…okay. I've been paying illegal immigrants to work for me. I…Mother helped me start my own business. I make specialized running shoes, but the cost of material…labor…parts…machines and…I was barely able to keep my head above water. Mother…she was so proud of me. I had orders pouring in from professional league teams all over the country, but I couldn't keep up…"

Ryan bowed his head in shame. "I got in over my head. I had to cut costs. My regular employees were demanding overtime payment…two delivery trucks started to have engine problems…the warehouse I was renting was costing me an arm and a leg. The money was draining fast and I couldn't keep up with the orders. I had to cut costs, so I fired all of my employees and hired a team of illegals who worked for

"It's all right, Jill," Sarah called out, struggling to sound confident. "Diaper number four has to be the correct diaper."

Amanda couldn't watch. She squeezed her eyes closed and went to her happy place—which was O'Mally's department store. "Never leaving home again…never leaving home again…" she began to hum.

Patty turned her head and looked at poor Jill. The poor woman was slowly breaking down into a slobbering, pathetic mess. Deep down, Patty liked Jill. After all, it was Jill who had hired her as a makeup artist when no other studio in town would give her the time of day. "I'll open the diaper for you!" she screamed. "Please, can't you see Jill is about to crash? Just leave her alone, you stupid clown!"

Sophia left the wooden post, marched over to Patty, and slapped her across the face. "Shut up!" she yelled and then pointed at Lyle. "Shoot Jill if she doesn't open the diaper in the next ten seconds!"

Lyle gave a curt nod. "Ten seconds, lady."

Jill began to shake all over. "Please…" she cried and then, realizing there was no escape, she lifted her right hand and reluctantly pulled a safety pin out of the backside of diaper number four. Jill yelled and threw her hands over her thin face, expecting to get sprayed with a deadly poison. Instead, a simple white envelope dropped down onto the floor. "What…" Jill said in a shocked voice. She looked down at the envelope and then broke out into tears. "No poison…I'm alive."

Sophia walked over to Jill, snatched up the envelope, and then ordered Lyle to imprison Jill back in her seat. Lyle grabbed Jill's arm and did as ordered.

"Okay, ladies and gentlemen," Sophia called out in a

voice that sounded upset but determined, "it appears that our contestants have lived through the first game and managed to secure the first clue." Sophia walked back to the wooden post, opened the envelope, and pulled out a piece of paper. "I hold in my hand the first clue that will point to the killer!"

Lyle, back at his station, grabbed the sound box and pressed a button. Applause and cheers raced across the stage. Sarah, who still couldn't see past all the bright lights enough to make out who was sitting in the studio audience, sat very still and waited for Sophia to continue.

"Stupid blokes," Amanda mumbled under her breath. "They'll get theirs."

"Yes, they will," Sarah whispered without Sophia hearing her.

Sophia raised the piece of paper in her hand like a flag. "Who is the real killer? Will this first clue tell the truth? There is only one way to find out." Sophia lowered the piece of paper and then danced over to Sarah. "Detective, will you do the honors?"

"I guess I have no other choice," Sarah told Sophia. Sophia grinned and dropped the piece of paper down onto Sarah's lap and then skipped away. Sarah picked up the piece of paper, struggling not to pull too much at her wrist, and then read the clue attached. The clue was typed in 12 point Arial font. Each typed letter was in bold, highlighted capitals with little knives darting everywhere. "*Guys are boring…it's a ladies' world…or is it?*"

A silent hush fell over everyone. After about five minutes, Ryan spoke. "So the killer is a woman, right?"

"It seems that way." Sarah nodded, uncertain how to apply

the clue to the situation. Did the clue imply the kil man or a woman? Sarah wasn't certain.

"Maybe you're the killer," Patty barked at Ryan After all, you killed our chance to ever be happy, you j

"Oh, go cry to Richie Stewart!" Ryan yelled feeling hot tears sting his eyes. He loved Patty more loved…his own mother. Patty was his world, his heart. Now he was losing the woman who completed heartbeat. "A gold-digging liar," he whispered a dropped from his eye. "You're nothing but a vicious li You're the one who destroyed our chance to be happy. it all planned."

"No, you had it all planned," Patty told Ryan ar down. "You're the one who has been—"

"Don't," Ryan begged. "Patty, you know what I doing has been for us."

"Really?" Patty asked as tears poured from h "Sometimes, Ryan, I wonder. I wonder if you rea what's the use. It's over."

Sophia saw a chance to increase her ratings. "Perha should tell us what little deeds he has been up to behi old mother's back?" she asked in a curious voice that s creepy and cruel. "Ryan, you have five minutes to co dear old Patty Darling is going to go open a diaper."

"What?" Ryan exclaimed. "But…that's not part game. We answered those stupid riddles. We found tl diaper."

Lyle threw a worried look at Sophia. The man in wouldn't appreciate having the rules changed. Sophia Lyle and continued. "You have five minutes, Ryai grinned.

pennies…families who worked around the clock. That's why I've been able to keep up with all of my orders. I'm sorry, Mother."

"I told you to let me help you," Patty cried. "Ryan, I wanted to help you…for us. But you insisted on shoving me to the side."

"Well," Sophia grinned, "I'm sure a load of ICE agents are rushing to your warehouse as we speak." Sophia clapped her hands. "Oh, the show keeps getting better and better."

Lyle watched angry and bitter comments arrive, aimed at Ryan. People were calling Ryan a savage and a coward. Ryan Mables had now become the enemy of over ten million people. Sophia, in one single stroke, had managed to destroy the man's life. Before Lyle could read any more comments, the cell phone sitting on the small table began to buzz. Lyle quickly grabbed the phone and read an angry text message. "Stay with the plan! No more games or else!" the text message read. Lyle slowly put the cell phone down and threw a quick hand at Sophia. "Commercial break," he called out in a voice that alerted Sophia's gut.

"We'll return in five minutes," she told her viewing audience and then watched Lyle push the tablet down at the floor and mute the volume. "What is it?" she demanded.

"Boss man isn't happy with what you're doing," Lyle informed Sophia in a worried tone. "Stay on track, okay?" Lyle showed Sophia the text.

Sophia folded her arms. "I'm simply making the show more interesting."

Lyle pointed at Sarah, Amanda, Jill, Patty, and Ryan. "You're creating a soap opera," he told Sophia. "Stick to the plan and play by the rules."

Sophia felt her cheeks turn red. She didn't like being told what to do—however, the man in charge was too powerful to stand toe-to-toe with; for now, at least. Sophia had plans of her own. "Very well," she hissed and then walked back to her hostages. "Game two will begin very soon," she promised. "If you thought game one was fun…just wait. Game two will be more intense…but don't worry, the poison powdered diapers…they're not going anywhere."

Sophia snatched up the diaper she had dropped onto Patty's lap and replaced it on the Diaper Rash game board. "I will have my killer one way or the other," she promised, turning to face five worried people. "In the end, I will have my revenge on everyone."

Chapter Nine

onrad rubbed his eyes with a tired hand and glanced down at a box of Chinese noodles sitting on his lap. "Sky clouded up but then cleared," he told Pete, "but it doesn't look like it's going to be that way again."

"Nope," Pete said with his elbow hanging out of the driver's side window of his old car. "Storms in Los Angeles are strange, angry things. They come out of nowhere, attack, and then wander off." Pete looked down at his own box of Chinese noodles. Sitting in his old car, parked beside an old studio building facing the studio Sarah was trapped in, watching a dark sky rumble and hiss, it felt like the old days. "Sarah has the situation under control, Conrad," he said in an easy voice. "I know my girl."

"Those riddles could have been deadly," Conrad told Pete. "That game could have taken a different turn and—"

"But Sarah won the game," Pete reminded Conrad. "As cops we can't go on the what-ifs. We have to take what we get and be grateful." Even though the day was hot, Pete grabbed a worn down brown travel mug and gulped down some coffee. "When I was a kid growing up in this town, I swore I was going to be John Wayne or Jimmy Stewart when I grew up. I was fascinated by these old studios."

Conrad turned his head and watched Pete shove his cigar into his mouth. "How did you end up becoming a cop?"

Pete glanced around at the people, commotion, and buildings standing before his eyes. "When I was sixteen my good friend Walker Natson was murdered. I won't get dramatic...I'll just say that my friend's death started a fire in me...a fire for justice." Pete's eyes filled with sorrowful memories. "Walker was a good kid...a church-going kid who helped old women cross the street and all that. He made good grades in school, had a pretty sweetheart...and then one day he was run down by a couple of drag racers...senseless."

"It always seems to be that way, doesn't it?" Conrad said. He reached for a cold soda, took a drink, and then debated on the Chinese noodles. "I guess I should eat." Pete nodded. Conrad opened the box of Chinese noodles and then went for a plastic fork. "The old days were simple," he told Pete, taking a bite of noodles. "I remember when I first became a cop... man, it was nothing like it is today."

"The world has changed for the worse," Pete agreed, allowing his eyes to walk around the studio lots. "Back in my day, we didn't even have computers. Today...everything is computers." Pete moved the half-smoked cigar to the corner of his mouth and took some more coffee down. "Back in my day, a man used his brain to solve crimes...today the computers do all the thinking...but," Pete nodded toward the studio Sarah was trapped in, "our girl isn't connected to a computer. Sarah is being forced to use her brains."

Conrad locked his eyes on the studio as a heavy raindrop fell from the dark sky and struck the windshield of Pete's old car. "Pete?"

"Yeah?"

"Sometimes I think…maybe it's time to leave Alaska, you know? I mean, Snow Falls is nothing more than a little stop in the road…a place for the polar bears." Conrad kept his eyes on the dark studio. "What type of life would our kid have in that town? It takes forever to drive south to Anchorage. All Snow Falls really has is O'Mally's department store." Pete shifted his eyes to Conrad and waited for the man to continue. "And then sometimes I think Snow Falls is the only place that's really safe for our kid, you know? Besides the freezing winds and bitter snow, Snow Falls isn't a bad little town."

"You missing New York?" Pete dared to ask.

"Miss New York?" Conrad asked and then laughed in a way that sounded sick. "Do I miss the corruption at city hall…the crime-ridden subways…the gangs…the overcrowded sidewalks…the pickpockets…paying ten dollars for a hot dog…" Conrad kept his eyes on the dark studio as his memory walked him back to the busy streets of New York. "Do I miss the murders and all the red tape? No way. I had my days of being a New York cop, and let me tell you, I don't miss it one bit. New York has become a puddle of sewage that attracts nothing but flies." Conrad finally turned his head and looked at Pete. "Mafia…corrupt politicians…bad cops…add those slime bags in with your regular everyday criminal and what do you get? A city that's so polluted with crime and corruption that it suffocates you."

"Los Angeles isn't much better," Pete pointed out. "At times I regret not buying that little cabin that was close to you and Sarah. But, as bad as it sounds, this city…I belong here. I belong at these studios…on the crowded highways…in the canyons…on the beach. I just wish Los Angeles was like it was in the old days. Now the city has transformed into some type of place you'd see in a science fiction movie where everything looks normal on the outside, but on the inside, where nobody can see, it's all Dr. Jekyll and Mr. Hyde."

Conrad watched a second raindrop strike the windshield and then a third. "I think Sarah misses Los Angeles, Pete."

"I know she does," Pete agreed.

Conrad sat silent for a minute. "Sarah could never leave Snow Falls."

"Nope," Pete said in a sad voice. "That gal is Alaska-bound." Pete waited for a fourth raindrop to fall. When it didn't arrive, he took a bite of noodles, somehow chewing with his half-smoked cigar still in his mouth, and then grabbed some coffee. "The Sarah I knew, Conrad…Detective Sarah Garland…she's still around, but not as much anymore. I miss that."

"Sarah killed the Snowman," Conrad told Pete. "She doesn't have nightmares anymore, you know. Now when Sarah wakes up, there's a peace to her. She's writing better than ever, too." Conrad checked his watch. Steve needed more time. "Sarah's publisher is excited about the new series that's in the works…and with our baby on the way, there's a peace in the air. I don't think Sarah wants to be a cop anymore."

"That's the part I have a hard time accepting," Pete sighed. "I miss my old partner. That girl was…and still is…something special." Pete put down his coffee. "I'm getting older, Conrad. Someday…maybe soon…I'll be forced to give up my gun and start taking long walks on the beach until my wife throws me into a nursing home." Pete shook his head. "All I ever do at home is sit around and watch old cop shows, missing the old days…wishing…remembering…wanting." Pete sighed. "My wife puts up with me because we've been married for over forty years, but I know she's ready for me to give up the life and move on."

"If I recall, your wife was excited about moving to Alaska," Conrad pointed out.

"Yeah…she sure was," Pete said in a guilt-ridden voice. "And stupid old Pete ruined it. Why? Because I can't let go of Los Angeles…of my life here." Pete removed the cigar from his mouth. "A man belongs in a certain place, Conrad. I belong in Los Angeles. I guess I'll die in this city and be buried in the old cemetery up in the canyon."

Conrad understood Pete's statement. Deep down, as much as he denied it to the world, he missed New York. As horrible as the city was…the bright lights at night, the sight of all the taxis, Broadway, Central Park in the wintertime… Coney Island…corn dogs…rides on the subway…little Italian restaurants…memories that were special…always lingered like a strong hand pulling him back. But it was like Pete said; the world has changed, and even though everything still appeared somewhat normal on the outside, on the inside, a deadly virus was overtaking the human heart. "I guess Sarah and I will grow old and be buried in Snow Falls someday."

"There's nothing wrong with that." Pete glanced into the backseat at a gray laptop. "Screen is still on break."

Conrad took a bite of noodles. "Sarah could have gotten off two clean shots by now," he told Pete. "There may be more clowns around, but so far all we've seen are two. Sarah could have easily taken those two clowns out." Conrad went for his soda. "I know Sarah. She's after the big fish."

"The clowns inside definitely had inside help," Pete agreed. "Right now, every single worker has been ordered to stand on tight lips by Mr. Earton or lose their jobs."

"Which leaves us with Steve," Conrad replied. He checked his watch again and then finished off his soda. "I hope this guy is good, Pete."

"I knew Steve's old man," Pete explained as a fourth raindrop finally struck the windshield. "If Steve is anything like his father, we're in good shape." Pete grabbed a pack of matches off the dashboard, lit his cigar, and looked around. "My gut is telling me that someone is out to destroy this studio," he continued. "Whoever is working behind the scenes wanted to make his attack public and is using social media to accomplish that mission."

"Any ideas?" Conrad asked.

Pete puffed on his cigar. "It's like I said, Conrad. Mr. Earton might own this studio but there are a lot of people behind the scenes that have their hands in his pockets. A man like Earton needs sponsors with lots of money." Pete motioned around at the lots and buildings. "Studios like this—protected by high fences, security guards, political covers—it's a perfect set to run drugs, guns, and other criminal garbage while throwing movies out at the public—"

"And television and game shows," Conrad added.

Pete nodded. "Studios like this one," he continued, "well, you better bet there's more going on underground than what's being seen above ground." Pete worked on his cigar. "I can probably bet my pension by telling you there's been a lot of murders that have taken place right at this very studio that the police aren't aware of—and don't want to be aware of."

"Yeah," Conrad said in a dark tone, "I bet there has been a lot of murders." He looked at the studio his wife was trapped in. "All I want is my wife back, safe and sound," he told Pete. "I also want Amanda back, safe and sound. It's taking everything I've got to keep Amanda's husband at the hotel. The guy is ready to storm the studio building barehanded…and so am I."

"Patience," Pete warned. "Conrad, my gut is telling me someone with a whole lot of power is working to take down Earton. Maybe this person wants Sun Waves Studio for himself? Who knows? All we can do right now is wait and see what Steve—"

"Someone mention my name?"

Pete turned his head and saw Steve approaching his old car. "Hop in the backseat, kid."

Steve slid into the backseat, spotted the laptop, and then quickly inserted a disk. "I worked fast," he explained in a quick, determined voice. "I managed to record a month's worth of security footage. It wasn't hard to hack the system, and I can go back even further if you need me to. In the meantime, chew on the food I just put into this laptop."

"You do work fast," Pete stated in an impressed voice. "I thought you would need more time."

"So did I," Steve confessed and then glanced around to make sure no one was watching. "Sometimes you catch a break," he explained. "Sometimes you hack into a system that's nothing but pancakes." Steve stared at the laptop. Suddenly the screen changed. "Hey, they're going live again," he announced. "I better get back to the van." Steve jumped out of the backseat and ran back to the cop van.

"Good guy," Conrad said in a grateful voice as he leaned over the back seat and grabbed the laptop. "Now let's see what's going on."

"You watch the show," Pete told Conrad as he ripped out the disk Steve had put into the laptop. "I'm going to take a walk to the van and view the goods." Pete rolled up the driver's side window and then grabbed his coffee. "Look," he told Conrad, "my gut is telling me the clowns inside are puppets. Whoever is working behind the scenes—"

"A really poisonous spider, right?" Conrad asked.

Pete nodded. "I need to go watch the goods."

Conrad watched Pete jump out into the shadowy day and vanish under the dark, stormy sky. "Don't worry, honey," he whispered, spotting Sarah's beautiful face appear on the laptop screen. "Pete and I are going to step on the spider who is weaving this web. In the meantime, you continue to play it real smart, okay?"

Although Sarah couldn't hear Conrad, her heart felt the man close by. "I can feel your love, sweetheart," she whispered and then looked at Sophia.

Lyle gave Sophia a thumbs-up. Sophia drew in a deep breath and then raised her hands into the air and waved at the tablet. "Welcome back," she exclaimed. "Our second game is about to begin, but first I want to take a few minutes to talk about a man who you may or may not know…a man who has destroyed the lives of innocent people in order to build his empire." Sophia glanced down at a piece of paper and studied a computer-printed itinerary. It was time to bring Mr. Earton into the big picture. Sophia walked over to Jill and patted the woman's left shoulder. "Jill Nayforth," she said, "would you like to tell the world what kind of slime ball criminal your daddy is or should I?"

Jill threw her eyes up at the creepy clown mask Sophia was wearing. "Leave me alone," she demanded, shaking violently. "You've ruined my career and my life. Isn't that enough, you… monster!"

"I guess that's a no," Sophia told her viewing audience in a disappointed voice and then skipped back to the wooden post. "I suppose I will tell the world just who Mr. Earton truly is. But first I want to present a list of names…well, more like a list of people Mr. Earton has murdered. This may come as a shock to my viewers, but we're all grown-ups, right? Sure, we are." Sophia raised a second piece of paper and showed it to the tablet.

A sixty-eight-year-old man wearing a gray suit that cost more money than Sophia would ever see in her lifetime raised a hard, vicious fist and struck a mahogany wood desk holding relics from the old days. "Shut them down!" he yelled.

Detective Wallace slowly placed his hands behind his back. "We can't, Mr. Earton…I'm sorry."

Mr. Earton sneered up at Detective Wallace and then went for an old brown phone sitting on his desk. It was time to make a call.

Chapter Ten

"On this list I have the names of fourteen men and women," Sophia announced. Lyle hit the sound box. Sounds of awe and terror floated into the air, accompanied by eerie music that gave Sarah the creeps. "The names on this list date back to 1978, nearly forty years ago. Mr. Earton was twenty-eight years old at that time in history." Sophia stepped out from behind the wooden post and pointed at the circle of five hostages. "And one of our contestants works for Mr. Earton…in the line of murder, that is." Lyle hit the sound box again. Sounds of anger and rage filled the stage. "I know, I know, it's horrible."

"What does it matter?" Ryan yelled. "You've destroyed our lives! Who cares who Mr. Earton has killed? Who cares which one of us is a killer?"

"He's right," Jill cried. "You've destroyed us all."

Amanda glanced at Sarah and then nodded down to the handcuffs. Sarah studied Sophia, saw the woman zooming in on Jill, and quickly glanced down at the handcuffs. To her shock, Amanda was slowly and patiently working her right hand free. The woman had small, fragile wrists that any pair of handcuffs would have a difficult time holding. "When she gets close enough…I slug her…you shoot her…and then shoot the other clown," she whispered to Sarah.

Sarah threw her eyes toward Lyle and struggled to see who was sitting out in the studio audience. So far, not a single sound or any sign of human movement had appeared out in the studio audience area, leading Sarah to believe that Sophia and Lyle were alone. But could there be more clowns around? "Not yet, June Bug," she whispered back at Amanda. "There could be more clowns around."

"How much longer, love?" Amanda begged. "We can't—"

"You two," Lyle yelled, "stop whispering!"

Sophia shot her eyes at Sarah and Amanda. "What are you two chatting about?" she demanded.

"Your wonderful outfit," Amanda responded in a sarcastic tone. "What do you think, genius? We're wondering how to escape this nightmare. I mean, really, do you really think we want to sit around all day and night with your ugly face and creepy clown voice? How stupid are you?"

Sophia narrowed her eyes, yanked out her gun, and approached Amanda. "You're a bug on the rug to me, London," she growled.

"Oh, go shove it in your ear," Amanda popped back. "Do you think you're something special…or scary…because you're wearing a cloak and a creepy clown mask? I've dealt with worse than you, sister." Amanda locked eyes with Sophia, struggling to see through the clown mask. "I'm the one who shot the Back Alley Killer, and I also tangled with his deranged daughter. But don't think that's all," Amanda added. "I've been infected with a deadly virus…punched a deadly model in the face…slugged a little weirdo…been strangled. This is a vacation compared to some of the nightmares I've been caught in. So do me a favor and stop acting like you're unique, sister, because all you are is a little weirdo wearing a creepy clown's mask…and trust me, you'll end up sleeping six feet under or wearing prison stripes."

Lyle waited for Sophia to explode. Amanda's daring rant was surely going to throw the woman into a fit of rage. Lyle wasn't wrong. Sophia began to lift her gun and aim it at Amanda, eyes dripping with murder. Amanda was prepared. She quickly lifted her legs and kicked Sophia right in the gut.

"Now!" Amanda yelled at Sarah as she yanked her wrist free.

Sarah watched Sophia stumble backward, hit the wooden post, topple over, and then crash down to the ground. Left with no choice but to act, she quickly used her free hand to yank the hidden gun out of the ankle holster and get a clean shot off at Lyle before the man could act. The last thing Lyle saw before losing his life was Sophia's crumpled body.

"Don't move!" Sarah hollered at Sophia as the woman began to struggle to her feet. Sarah fired a warning shot in the air. "My other hand may be handcuffed, but I can get a clear shot at you!"

Sophia froze. Where was her gun? She looked around and saw Lyle lying down on his face. "Lyle?" she called out. "Lyle?" Lyle didn't answer. "What have you done?" Sophia screamed as her eyes spotted her gun lying a few feet away. "What have you done!"

"Don't move!" Sarah warned Sophia, waiting to see if other clowns would soon appear with guns blazing. "Get your hands in the air!"

Sophia ignored Sarah. Her mind and heart were filled with too much blind rage to listen. "You're dead!" she screamed and dove at her gun. Sarah, left with no choice but to shoot, fired off two single shots that carried Sophia into a darkness the woman would never escape from.

"Everyone, stand up and form a line," she ordered. Amanda, Jill, Patty, and Ryan quickly stood up and did as Sarah said. "We're going to get out of here. Follow me." Sarah looked out into the studio audience area; just as she suspected, the "people" she thought she saw were mere silhouettes. She moved the line over to Lyle and began searching the dead man's pockets. She located the handcuff key, freed everyone, and then threw her eyes at the tablet. "Conrad, honey, I know you're watching. I overheard the woman clown talking about a secret exit that's under the backstage. We're going to locate that exit. I don't know if there are any more clowns around…it doesn't seem to be that way. Please…stand clear of the studio…the bombs could go off at any minute. I'm certain the two clowns I just killed are working for someone who might be able to activate the bombs!"

With those words, Sarah led Amanda, Jill, Patty, and Ryan backstage. The backstage area was dark. "Everyone, help me pull back the main curtain…we need light."

"You heard the lady!" Amanda yelled. "Let's move."

Jill, Patty, and Ryan all grabbed the main curtain and, with the help of Sarah and Amanda, managed to pull the curtain back. Bright light spilled into the backstage area, creating a world of hope rather than fear and doubt. "The passage could be anywhere," Jill said in a shaky voice. "We need to escape through one of the main doors."

"That could activate the bombs," Sarah informed Jill,

searching the wooden floor with sharp eyes. "Look," she said, "if anyone knows something I don't, now would be the time. Those two clowns I killed aren't working alone."

Patty and Ryan threw their eyes at Jill. "She would know more than us," Patty told Sarah in a scared, impatient voice. "I've only been working at this studio for about five months. I still have trouble finding my way around."

"Well, what about it?" Amanda pressed at Jill. "Look, I want to live long enough to have my bedtime cup of tea, okay?"

Sarah quickly walked over to Jill. "Jill," she said, forcing calmness to her voice, "I don't care what happened earlier. I don't care what that clown said or who she was. Your life… your reasons…that's your personal business. All I want to do is live long enough to have my baby…please."

Jill looked into Sarah's pleading eyes and felt her heart finally surrender. "There is…a hidden passage," she confessed. "I…please…you don't understand…"

"In time," Sarah promised. "No one is judging you, Jill. We're all here to help each other."

Jill felt tears begin to fall from her eyes. "Follow me," she whispered in a broken voice.

"Now we're talking," Amanda said in a relieved voice and quickly followed Jill to the far northern corner of the floor. Jill pointed down at the floor and explained that underneath the floorboards was a hidden trap door that opened up to a hidden tunnel that ran under the studio and came out to an abandoned back lot.

"What are we waiting for?" Amanda asked.

"Get the floorboards removed," Sarah told Amanda in an urgent voice and then ran back to the front stage and made her way to the tablet. "Conrad, we've located the exit. We're going to take a tunnel that ends up in an abandoned lot on the northern end of the studio. Meet me there."

Sarah threw her eyes at Sophia and Lyle and decided to check the bodies. If the person pulling the strings wanted to detonate the three bombs, he…or she…would have by now. "Let's see…" Sarah hurried to check Lyle's pockets and, to her relief, found the switch that detonated the bombs—but that didn't mean a hidden person didn't have a second switch. She carefully placed the switch into the front pocket of her dress and continued on.

"Love?"

Sarah threw her head backward and saw Amanda running toward her. "June Bug, you should be—"

"Standing at your side," Amanda informed Sarah. "Our three friends are pulling up the floorboards."

Sarah felt a great love for Amanda swell up in her heart. "Okay…check the dead woman and gather the papers off the wooden post."

"Got it!" Amanda ran to Sophia and began searching the woman's pockets. She found hidden papers but nothing else. "I found some papers!" she informed Sarah and then hurried to gather the papers that were sitting on the wooden post.

Sarah stood up and stepped in front of the tablet. "Conrad, I've located three guns, a bomb switch…a disk…a wallet…and a set of keys, along with two cell phones and a laptop. We're leaving this tablet behind," she explained. "Amanda and I are moving out…meet us at the abandoned lot." Sarah handed Amanda one of the guns she had located and then ran to the backstage area just in time to see Ryan pulling up an old wooden trap door sitting on rusted hinges. "We need light!" Sarah said.

"Our cell phones!" Amanda called out.

Jill, Patty, and Ryan all yanked out their cell phones. Sarah shifted the laptop she had tucked under her right arm to her left arm. "Ryan, lead the way. Patty, you follow. Jill, go third. Amanda and I will cover the rear. Let's move."

Ryan threw a hard eye at Patty. "I should leave you here," he said in a sour, angry voice and then dropped down onto all fours and looked down into the dark hole. As he did, a hand exploded out of the darkness, grabbed Ryan by the hair, and yanked him down into the abyss.

"Ryan!" Patty screamed. "Ryan!"

Sarah dropped the laptop, dropped down onto one knee, and aimed the gun she was holding at the black hole. "Everyone, get back!" she hollered.

Amanda grabbed Jill and pulled her away from the trap door. Patty hesitantly followed. "Stay," Amanda begged and then raced to Sarah's side, hit one knee, and aimed the gun Sarah had given her at the trap door. "Okay…now what, love?" she asked in a shaky voice. "Someone…or something is down there."

Sarah studied the dark hole. "You down there…speak to me!"

"I have a bomb switch, too, Detective," a creepy voice floated out of the dark hole. "If you try to leave the building… boom. Now, close the trap door or I will put a bullet into this young man!"

"Patty…run!" Ryan tried to holler but his voice was quickly cut off with a hard sound that Sarah was familiar with. Ryan had been hit in the back of the head with a gun.

"Close the trap door, Detective, and stay inside the studio…or else," the voice warned. "And go back to the front stage and tell the world what has happened. Tell them that if they try to enter the tunnel from the far end…boom."

Sarah stared at the dark hole with desperate eyes. What in the world was going on? "All right…" she said. She handed Amanda her gun and, using all the strength her exhausted body could muster, closed the trap door. As soon as the trap door snapped closed, the cell phone she had taken off Sophia's body rang. Sarah quickly answered. "I closed the trap door—"

"Stay on the main stage where I can see you," the voice warned. "If you try to leave, I will detonate the bombs…and no calls in or out of the studio…or else. I'll be in touch."

Sarah heard the call end, looked at Amanda with confused eyes, and then sighed. "Everyone…back onto the main stage," she said and, on weak legs, moved back to the main stage and approached the tablet.

"Conrad…honey…there has been a change of plans. Someone was waiting in the tunnel. He has Ryan Mables as a hostage. I've been ordered to stand down and wait. If I try to escape, the bombs will detonate. Stand down and wait. Do not let anyone try to enter through the far end of the tunnel located on the abandoned lot."

Amanda stepped next to Sarah. "Uh…hi, hubby." She waved and made a painful face. "As you can see, I'm still alive…and…well, I hope you're not too mad. I mean, how was I supposed to know a bunch of crazy Yanks were going to pull a scheme like this? Anyway, I promise from now on I'll stay in Alaska and spend my days shopping at O'Mally's, okay, dear?"

Sarah put her arm around Amanda, walked her back to the circle of chairs, and sat down. "You know, June Bug," she said and pointed at the two dead clowns, "this case just keeps getting stranger by the minute."

Amanda tossed a cautious eye up at Jill and Patty. "I know, love," she whispered, "and the horrible fact is…we have a killer among us…and I don't think the killer is Ryan Mables."

Sarah lifted her eyes and studied Jill's thin, broken face and then focused on Patty. Patty was staring down at the stage floor with tears dropping from her eyes. Both women appeared weak, frightened, and defeated…or was their appearance only an act? After all, Sarah was in the womb of a movie studio where reality was fiction and fiction was reality.

"June Bug," Sarah whispered, "if we ever try to leave Alaska again…have someone admit us to a mental home."

Amanda grinned. "Love," she promised, "if I ever try to leave home again, just slug me."

"Deal," Sarah whispered and locked her eyes on Jill and Patty again. What in the world was going on? Sarah didn't know but she had a gut feeling that before the approaching night ended, she would have all the answers her heart needed.

Chapter Eleven

"Take those ugly masks off," Patty demanded in an angry voice. "Let's see who those two monsters are."

Sarah shook her head no. "The police will unmask them," she warned, keeping her eyes aimed at the backstage area. She imagined a hideous dead clown slithering up through the hidden trap door wearing hungry fangs and glowing red eyes. Of course that type of stuff was silly images pathetic horror movies created—horror movies made by unholy minds. In reality a man of flesh and blood was hiding under the studio floor; a man that a bullet could easily destroy. Still, being pregnant, confused, angry, and hungry all at the same time didn't soothe Sarah's overactive imagination. "There are protocols to follow."

"Ryan may be dead!" Patty shouted at Sarah, fully aware that the tablet was still up and running—fully operational—broadcasting the event to a viewing audience that had nearly doubled in size. Obviously, gun play, two dead clowns, and a mystery monster hiding under the studio was a lot better than cable television (of course TV was trash in itself, but still, watching the viewing audience double in size worried Sarah). "We could all die at any second…and if I'm going to die, I want to see who those two clowns are."

"Back off right now!" Sarah growled at Patty and raised a firm and angry finger at the girl. "I'm not showing the world who those two clowns are, is that clear? Right now, we have a missing person, an unknown subject who claims to have a bomb switch, two dead terrorists, and a very hungry pregnant woman…so don't push me, girl, or I'll knock you into yesterday!"

Sarah turned to the tablet, feeling foolish. After killing Sophia and Lyle, panic had overwhelmed her sense of calmness. Worried that whoever was pulling the strings might detonate the bombs, Sarah, with the help of Amanda, had searched the two dead bodies, located different items, and then—after Sarah had spoken into the tablet hoping Conrad was watching instead of calling her husband—they had made a futile attempt to escape. The escape attempt had ended in disaster.

"Conrad, honey, I should have called you…but I panicked. I wasn't sure if the bombs were going to detonate or not. I…I'm trying to put the pieces together, but I think this is one case that is going to…cook my goose." Sarah deliberately cast a shadow over her retired badge in order to make herself appear weak and defeated. "All I can do is wait…"

Pete grinned. "You're doing good, kiddo," he said, patting Steve on his shoulder, and then stepped out into a hard, dark falling rain that had turned the late day into an early form of night. The rain struck Pete's overcoat with familiar sounds and said hello. Pete quickly glanced up at a stormy sky that wasn't going anywhere soon, nodded, and walked back to his old car, where he found Conrad sitting in the passenger seat holding a laptop.

"Old stage tunnels…sewer tunnels…fire escape tunnels…" he told Conrad, sitting down in the driver's seat. "You name it…this studio has it."

Conrad kept his eyes on Sarah's beautiful face. "I assumed," he said in a tired, worried voice without looking at Pete. "You've finished watching the security footage?"

Pete nodded. "A lot of night activity made by two people," he explained. "I was expecting a crowd of intruders, but that isn't the case." Pete watched the hard-falling rain strike the windshield of his old car and thought about the canyons for a minute. The canyons captivated his mind—especially in the rain. "Movies…books…have a way of changing how a man looks at things," he told Conrad. "Right now, I feel like I'm trapped inside of an old black-and-white creepy detective movie."

"You're not the only one," Conrad assured Pete. "My wife had to shoot two terrorists wearing clown masks dead. I can't imagine what's going through her mind right now."

"Sarah is a tough cop," Pete promised Conrad. "She understands how to react and how to deal with the flood that follows."

"You mean nightmares."

"What cop doesn't have nightmares?" Pete asked. "Sarah can handle this."

"Pregnant?" Conrad demanded, finally taking his eyes off

Sarah's worried face and looking at Pete. "Is it fair for a pregnant woman to—"

"Life isn't fair, Conrad," Pete cut him off with a quick bark. "I don't want to hear a bunch of miserable, whiny what-ifs, do you hear me? Sarah is a tough cop and she can handle this, got me?"

"Yeah, Pete, I got you." Conrad steadied his mind. "Okay, so…two people, right?"

"A woman and a man," Pete said. "Steve is getting more footage, but from what I watched, for the last month, every night at midnight, the woman and man arrived like clockwork in a black van, were let inside the studio by the same security guard, and drove to the studio Sarah and Amanda are trapped in. They always parked out of view of the security camera that watches the studio…and don't appear again until about half an hour before sunrise."

"The security guard—"

"Quit without notice yesterday," Pete informed Conrad. "Most likely some working stiff who took a huge payoff to look the other way for a while."

"The studio—"

"The studio in question closed shop every day at seven sharp," Pete continued. "By midnight nothing but stage bats were hanging around." Pete took the half-smoked cigar he was chewing on out of his mouth, studied it, and then tossed the cigar onto the dashboard. "The two clowns Sarah shot down appear to be our two night owls," he continued. "Two night owls, by the way, who spent more than a month planning this event."

"Which means—"

"The three bombs aren't going to be easily detectable," Pete said. "My guess is the three bombs sitting inside that studio are either up in the heat and air ducts or under the floors… maybe both."

Conrad walked his eyes back to the dark studio building. "Three bombs in a building that size…we're not talking about little firecrackers, Pete."

"Nope." Pete went for the cigar out of habit, even though he had just discarded it. "The man under the studio knows his stuff," he told Conrad. "Earton wasn't aware of what was taking place right under his nose…"

Conrad studied Pete's thoughtful face. "Who are we talking about, Pete?"

"I'm not sure," Pete confessed. "At first I thought we were talking about a major player…someone who is popular in the eyes of the world. But now…could it be that we're talking about a personal vendetta? Someone who has a lot of money… and wants revenge on Earton? And if that's the case, and I believe it is, why? What did Earton do to earn himself such an enemy? How are the two clowns involved?"

"The clowns appeared to be after a killer," Conrad pointed out.

"Which might connect Earton to a murder," Pete added. "Word around the studio is that Earton is locked up tight in his office and is refusing to speak to anyone except Wallace."

Conrad walked his eyes back to the laptop and spotted Sarah and Amanda standing off in the distance talking. "Is the SWAT team—"

"Wallace has ordered everyone to stand clear of the back lot."

"What?" Conrad asked in a shocked voice. "Pete, you're

kidding me, right? The SWAT team should be in a secure, hidden position covering the—"

"I know, Conrad," Pete said in a calm tone. "You're not talking to a greenhorn. But the problem is Wallace doesn't have a spine. That guy will do whatever Earton barks at him to do."

"Then it looks like I'm going—"

"Hold it," Pete said in a quick voice as Conrad went for his gun. "Stand down."

"My wife—"

"Is a smart cop," Pete reminded Conrad and then tossed a thumb at the storm. "Wallace has the back lot completely blocked off. If you try to sneak back there, every black-and-white on the force will mow you down."

Frustration ripped into Conrad's heart. "Pete, my wife is in danger and all I've been doing is sitting here—"

"Doing what a good cop is supposed to be doing," Pete assured Conrad and drew in a deep breath. "I'm on your side, remember? Don't bite at my ankles, okay? We're on the same team."

"I know we are."

Pete took a few seconds to study the storm and focus. "Leah Mayes seems to be a random target," he said in a voice that caught Conrad's attention.

"We've already established that fact…right?" Conrad asked with a frown.

Pete shrugged. "Earton is threatening to sue any media outlet that tries to dig into the past of Leah Mayes."

"Which means—"

"Leah Mayes was connected to Earton in a deeper way," Pete confirmed. "How? I don't know. What I do know is that the poison that killed that girl—according to a friend of mine that works over at the college—wasn't made in somebody's kitchen."

"I'm all ears."

"The poison is laced with an acid, right?" Pete asked.

Conrad nodded. "Yes, according to Sarah."

"The acid isn't felt at first…but eventually burns into the victim's skin," Pete continued. "We're talking about a time-released acid that acts to support the poison." Pete tapped the watch he was wearing. "Conrad, we've both run the minutes between the time of the first break and the time Leah Mayes kicked the can. We're talking about a weapon that was created by someone who understands chemistry up and down."

"Pete, that could be anyone."

"Earton has a brother," Pete told Conrad, staying on track. "A man named Patrick Earton. I'm having Steve run the man as we speak. The only problem is," Pete added in a careful voice, "Patrick Earton is supposed to have died in a car accident two years ago."

Conrad knew where Pete was going. "Earton tried to kill his own brother?"

"Could be," Pete said. "Could be that Ryan Mables, Patty Darling, or Jill Nayforth was the person who ran the man off the road. It could also be that Patrick Earton has a daughter…"

"A daughter?"

"A girl by the name of Sophia Johnson," Pete explained. "Linda Johnson divorced Patrick Earton while pregnant with her daughter." Pete took the cigar he was chewing on out of his mouth, studied it, and then continued. "That's as far as

Steve has gotten so far. I'll check back with him in an hour or so."

Conrad rubbed his chin. "Pete, you could be onto something," he said in a deep, thoughtful voice. "I wish there was a way to talk with Sarah."

"Sarah isn't allowed to make calls…maybe we can text her?" Pete suggested in an uneasy voice. "I'd hate to put her in danger."

Conrad thought for a minute. "Let's wait and see what Steve digs up before we make that decision."

"Smart man," Pete said. He looked through the rain toward the dark studio and then checked his watch. "I want to check in with Wallace," he told Conrad. "Wallace may not have a spine, but he's a good friend. Maybe I can squeeze some information out of him."

"How will you get into Earton's office?"

"I won't," Pete said in a disgusted voice. "I'll make Wallace come out to me."

Conrad locked his eyes on the laptop. Sarah and Amanda were still standing in the distance talking. Patty was sitting in a chair with her arms crossed, staring off toward the studio audience area. Jill was standing close to the tablet, nervously biting at her thumbnail. "Anyone could be the killer," he told Pete. "But you know…I've already placed my bet."

"Oh?" Pete asked.

Conrad nodded. "My bet is on Ryan Mables."

Pete grinned. "You read my mind," he told Conrad and slapped the man's shoulder. "I guess not all New York cops are lame brains."

"Not all," Conrad said, smirking. He forced his eyes away

from Sarah and focused on Pete. "Ryan Mables was hurting for money."

"And right now, as we speak, Detective Mel McNeston is roaming through Ryan Mables's shoe factory," Pete informed Conrad, even though Conrad was already aware of that fact. "Mel is a…well, let's say seaweed has more brains than that man…and he's not the type to stay honest, either…which makes me wonder why the higher-ups assigned him to the case."

"Exactly," Conrad agreed. "But, Pete, I don't think Ryan just happened to meet someone with some push and power."

"Patty Darling?" Pete asked.

Conrad nodded again. "Patty Darling…but the question is…could she be connected?" Conrad let his eyes float out to the storm. "If Patrick Earton is our man, we have to connect Patty Darling to him. She could be the bridge between Patrick Earton and Ryan Mables."

"Now you're thinking," Pete congratulated Conrad. "Now we're riding on the same brain waves."

Conrad rubbed his chin again. "Jill Nayforth might not be in the clear."

"Nope."

Conrad turned his head and looked at Pete. "You have a theory?"

"Yep," Pete stated and then decided to light his cigar and take a puff or two before jumping back out into the rain. "Jill Nayforth is the daughter of Earton, right?"

"That's the information that the dead clown claimed," Conrad agreed.

"Which means Jill Nayforth might have wanted her dear old daddy out of the way…with the promise from her dear old uncle that she would be given a nice little bonus if the woman joined his team," Pete explained. "I did a little digging and found out that Jill Nayforth's husband filed for divorce two years ago, about the same time Patrick Earton supposedly died in a car accident. Is that a connection? I'm not sure."

"Do we know who Jill Nayforth was married to?" Conrad asked.

Pete grinned. "Tony Nayforth...a writer," he answered Conrad and then added: "A writer who worked for Sun Waves Studio."

Conrad stared at Pete. "I'm assuming, by the tone of your voice—"

"Tony Nayforth relocated to New York soon after he divorced Jill," Pete told Conrad and took a puff on his cigar. "Earton personally fired the man...or threatened the man... depends on how you look at it."

"Can we contact Tony Nayforth?" Conrad asked.

Pete grinned. "I already have an old friend assigned to that task," he promised and then patted Conrad on the shoulder. "Your job is to sit tight and keep your eyes on our girl."

Conrad focused back on the laptop and then stiffened when he saw Sarah reach for her cell phone. "Hey, Pete, we have an incoming call...sit tight."

Chapter Twelve

Patrick Earton prepared to call Sarah from inside a hidden office sitting under Sun Waves Studio. The office had originally belonged to Dylan Paulerson, the man who had bought countless acres of land during the Great Depression and began construction on the new Golden Curtains Studio. The Golden Curtains Studio had stood until the late 1970s, when it was destroyed—intentionally or by accident—by a major fire that demolished sixty percent of the buildings, forcing the current owner, a man named Lyle Paulerson, Dylan Paulerson's grandson, to file for bankruptcy. It was around this time that Patrick's brother came into the picture and became involved with a man named Jones Bipstar, a dangerous and corrupt politician who bought the ruined Golden Curtains Studio and began building the Sun Waves Studio. But instead of having the old studio completely torn down, Jones Bipstar paid a great deal of money to have tons of dirt laid over the old studio and a large, next-to-impossible concrete floor created; underneath the concrete and dirt, Jones had secret tunnels installed that led to one unburned building after another, creating an underground gun smuggling operation that defeated the Feds. Millions upon millions of dollars had been poured into creating the underground operation center.

In 1994, Patrick's brother decided it was time to take control of the helm. He secretly killed off his opponents, hid their bodies underground, and took over, becoming partners with Joey DeDonato, a dangerous mafia boss in New York. But in 2011, Joey was killed and the entire gun-smuggling operation, which was bringing in millions each month, came to a halt. Patrick's brother was forced to rely on the studio he owned to make him money, forced to become an honest man —or so it seemed to the Feds. Instead of running guns, Patrick's brother turned to creating a drug smuggling operation—an operation that allowed Patrick to slowly start gaining power over his brother.

"Comfortable?" Patrick asked Ryan in a cold voice.

Ryan was now handcuffed and sitting on an old wooden chair facing a desk that, remarkably—even though it had been built in 1933—still had a clean shine to it. As a matter of fact, the entire office Ryan was being held captive in was remarkably fancy; lush carpet, burgundy walls, antique furnishings. Ryan wasn't shocked. Patrick used the office as his own personal headquarters that his brother wasn't aware of. Because Patrick's brother was claustrophobic, the man rarely ventured underground, allowing Patrick room to play.

"Why are you doing this?" Ryan asked, struggling to stay calm even though he was pretty certain Patrick was going to kill him.

Patrick stared at Ryan with deadly eyes. He was a man in his early sixties who was accustomed to violence, betrayal, and even murder. "My plan was working perfectly until Sarah Garland stepped into the picture. That…woman…killed my daughter…ruined my plans." Patrick folded his arms over a black suit that matched his soulless face. "I'm left with no other option but…to compromise."

"Compromise?" Ryan asked. "Mr. Earton, I did everything you asked. I had the illegals working at my factory run the drugs and—"

"I'm fully aware of what is taking place at the factory, boy," Patrick snapped. "Why do you think I changed locations?"

Ryan struggled to make sense of the situation. Patrick had caught Patty popping powerful pain pills in a private dressing room. Patrick gave Patty a choice: work for him or die. Patty accepted the first choice and began running drugs out of the studio for Patrick. A few months later, Ryan showed up at the studio to visit Patty. Patrick watched the meeting take place and learned that Ryan was in a tight financial squeeze. That's when he approached Ryan and ordered him to fire all of his employees—employees who were replaced by illegal aliens—and start running drugs from his factory in order to take some heat off the studio. Ryan had no choice but to agree to the offer—without Patty knowing.

"But why…I mean…that woman…she twisted my arm to make me confess—"

"Exactly," Patrick fired at Ryan and snapped up a fancy cigar out of a silver cigar dish. "This is all about taking down my brother. You are…a pawn. And may I remind you that 'woman' was my daughter." With those words, Patrick shoved the cigar into his mouth, grabbed a cell phone, and called Sarah. Sarah picked up on the first ring. Patrick quickly glanced at the computer screen attached to the right office wall and saw Sarah turn and face the tablet. "Have you had time to think, Detective?"

"I have," Sarah informed Patrick.

"I will detonate the bombs if you try to escape," Patrick warned. "And in your…condition…I wouldn't advise such a move."

Sarah stared at the tablet. Patrick was watching her—and so were over ten million viewers. Sarah knew she had to play it smart. "You have the upper hand. Please, just don't hurt my baby," she begged. "I'm not even a cop anymore. I'm retired."

"You still know how to use a gun," Patrick pointed out. "You killed two very important people."

"I wasn't given a choice."

"We all have choices," Patrick growled. "But I digress." Patrick chewed on the cigar in his mouth. "Detective, you are going to become a news reporter."

"A news reporter?" Sarah asked, pretending to sound confused. "Look, whoever you are, hasn't this gone far enough? Two people are dead…there doesn't need to be any more—"

"My daughter is dead," Patrick informed Sarah in a voice that sent a cold chill down Sarah's spine—a voice that told Sarah that Patrick had no intention of letting her leave the studio alive. "You killed my daughter and a man I wanted to call my son-in-law."

"Your daughter?" Sarah asked and threw a quick eye at Amanda. Amanda hurried over to Sarah. "Who are you?"

"You're smart…figure it out," Patrick ordered Sarah. "In the meantime I want you to start talking about how the owner of Sun Waves Studio, Mr. Earton himself, was once involved in a gun-smuggling scheme…how he killed more than eight men…and how he is now running drugs."

Sarah soaked in Patrick's words. "Okay."

Patrick chewed on his cigar for a minute. "I will have my revenge, Detective," he assured Sarah. "Jill Nayforth, Patty Darling, or Ryan Mables tried to kill me—but I will handle that part of the program in due time. Right now, we will focus entirely on the matter at hand." Patrick glared at Ryan. "I want to tell the viewers about a man named Albert Hinge."

"Albert Hinge?"

"Yes," Patrick said. "Albert Hinge is Mr. Earton's righthand man. Albert Hinge is connected to a man named Jose Garcia."

"Jose Garcia?" Sarah whispered as her mind dived into a pool of memories. "Yes…Jose Garcia…"

"Jose Garcia is currently in prison…well, controlling a prison…in Mexico," Patrick continued. "The rat is running drugs straight from his prison cell. He controls the guards, the prisoners. No one dares challenge this rat, not even Mr. Earton, who is running some very serious drugs through the studio. But rest assured, Detective, I'm challenging Jose Garcia. You will mention the rat's name, connect him to Mr. Earton, and report the information I relay to you. Is that clear?"

"What choice do I have?" Sarah asked. She glanced at Jill and Patty, saw the two women staring at her with nervous eyes, and shook her head. "You're not going to let us live, are you?"

"I will if you do as ordered."

"No," Sarah objected. "You're lying…I'm not stupid." Sarah closed her eyes, hoping to appear shaken and weak. "Please, at least let me call my husband. I…if you refuse… then no deal…just go ahead and blow us up." Sarah winced and waited, even though on the inside she was confident the strange man on the phone had no intention of detonating the bombs; not yet, at least. Whoever Sarah was speaking to needed her alive to broadcast very dangerous news. With the two clowns dead, no one else was left.

Patrick studied Sarah's lovely but scared face. He needed the woman alive…and willing to be his voice. "All calls will be made in front of the tablet in order for me to hear them," he ordered. "Each call will last for three minutes. Is that clear?"

"Fair enough," Sarah answered in a relieved voice.

"Each call will be on speakerphone."

Sarah sighed. So much for privacy. "No deal." She shook her head. "I'm not going to let the world hear a private conversation I need to have with my husband. Detonate the bombs if you must, but no deal."

"Love?" Amanda said with wide, terrified eyes. "Are you sure you know what you're doing?"

"What are you…nuts?" Patty screamed and ran at Sarah. "Who are you—"

"Back down," Sarah ordered in a stern tone, pointing at Patty. She told the girl if she took one step closer, she would end up in a body cast. Patty glared at Sarah with rage-filled eyes but backed down. "Whoever you are," Sarah told Patrick, "I demand privacy. If you agree, I will be your voice. I…what does it matter anyway? You're not going to let us leave this studio alive."

Patrick threw his eyes around the office. It was located in an underground building that a single tunnel connected to—a tunnel that Patrick had designed. The tunnel connected straight to the building his brother's office was located in— even though not a single other person, not even Mr. Earton, was aware of the tunnel. Patrick had destroyed the old tunnel, leading his brother to believe that the old building that had been used as a secret headquarters had finally been ruined by a cave-in.

Surely, Patrick thought, even if Sarah managed to sneak a plan past him…even if the cops did manage to break into the back tunnel…so what? No one could locate the tunnel he had created. Only one secondary tunnel connected to the tunnel Patrick had created. That was a problem because the secondary tunnel was part of a chain of other hidden tunnels. But the secondary tunnel that connected to the tunnel Patrick had designed was in itself very complicated to locate. Even if the police did somehow locate the tunnel, Patrick knew he would have plenty of time to escape—or would he? These complicated thoughts coursed through his mind as he evaluated Sarah's demand. "No speakerphone, but you will make your calls standing in front of the tablet," he ordered.

"Deal," Sarah said. "I will call my husband after we end this call. I want to speak to him before I start work."

Patrick walked his eyes to Ryan. "The games are just beginning, Detective," he promised. "You can try to play your games, but I promise you, in the end, I will win." Patrick spit out his cigar. "You killed my daughter…and for that, you will pay."

"I want to call my husband."

"Three minutes," Patrick snapped and ended the call.

Sarah quickly opened her eyes, shook her head at Amanda, and called Conrad. "Hey, honey, it's me. I have three minutes."

Conrad could have melted into Sarah's voice. "Okay, honey, pay close attention," he said and began filling Sarah's ears full. "That's where Pete and I are at right now."

"I don't think we're going to make it out of here alive,"

Sarah replied, pretending to sound broken. "This man said I killed his daughter."

"Sophia Johnson," Conrad said.

"I…did what any cop would do. Please don't be angry at me," Sarah told Conrad, allowing tears to fall from her worried eyes. "My three minutes are almost up," she said and checked the time on her cell phone. "I love you…and remember…beep."

"Beep?" Conrad asked.

"I love you…forever," Sarah whispered and ended the call. "Amanda, you better call your hubby. You have three minutes."

Amanda wiped at Sarah's tears. "I suppose I should, love," she said in a sad voice.

Sarah handed Amanda her cell phone and walked over to Patty and Jill. "Is there anyone you want to call?" she asked.

"No," Jill answered in a shaky voice. "All I want is a cigarette. I quit smoking…but I sure could use a cigarette right now."

Sarah studied Patty's face. "I suppose you could go for whatever type drug you were using, right?" she asked. Patty shot Sarah a vicious eye. Sarah quickly held up her right hand. "How long have you been clean, Patty…a few months?"

"My brother helped me get clean," Patty told Sarah in a voice that could have torn down brick walls. "I love Ryan… but his mother knew I was using. I wanted to prove to that old bat that she was wrong…that I wasn't a loser. Richie helped me get clean…happy?"

"Richie is your brother?" Sarah asked.

"Yeah," Patty finally caved. What did she have to lose? Her chance of living was slim to none. "Richie Stewart is my brother, okay…and he's a good guy. I mean, he has his problems…who doesn't? But deep down, Richie is okay." What Patty didn't tell Sarah was that Richie had been helping her run drugs for Patrick before Ryan came onto the scene. Patrick had continued to use Richie's services after hiring Ryan, without Patty's knowledge. Patty had assumed Patrick had cut her brother loose. "I was addicted to pain pills… Richie helped me kick the habit."

"Brother?" Ryan asked, sitting under Patty's feet. "So that's it…I should have known."

Patrick glared at Ryan, taking his focus off Sarah—and Amanda, who was talking on the phone, standing at an angle making it hard for him to see the woman's face. No matter, the woman was an idiot. Sarah was the smart one; or so Patrick assumed. What Patrick didn't know as he looked at Ryan and then focused his eyes back on Sarah was that Amanda wasn't speaking to her husband. No, Amanda was speaking with Pete and Pete was sure happy about the call.

"That's my opinion," Amanda whispered.

Pete hurried into a damp, dark stairwell and sat down on a wooden step. "Amanda, I need facts, not an opinion."

Amanda touched her nose and pretended to start crying. "It is a fact…I do love you," she whimpered.

"Good girl," Pete comforted Amanda. "You're a great cop and I'm very proud of your strength."

"I better get off the phone," Amanda continued to whimper. Amanda ended the call and walked over to Sarah, keeping her back to the tablet. "My parakeet Pete is a very smart bird," she told Sarah and offered a faint smile. Sarah studied Amanda's eyes and then nearly passed out. Amanda nodded. "It's a chance, love…but I know what my gut…and your gut…is telling you. All we can do now is wait and play the game, right?"

Sarah carefully took her cell phone back from Amanda. "And take down some bad guys in the meantime," she whispered. She tossed her eyes at the two dead clowns and then looked back at her best friend. "June Bug, remind me to crown you queen."

Amanda blushed. Being queen would be just fine with her.

Chapter Thirteen

Sarah and Amanda dragged a chair in front of the tablet. "Okay, love, buy us some time," Amanda whispered in Sarah's ear, pretending to issue a hug, and then wandered back to the circle of chairs Jill and Patty were at. Sarah stationed herself in the chair, softly touched her tender belly, and focused on the tablet. She knew Conrad was watching her every move and prayed the man understood the code word "beep."

Outside in the storm Conrad was making his way to the cop van Steve was housed in on legs that were full of new hope and energy. "Steve," Conrad called out as he bounced into the van soaked with rain. "I—"

"I know what you're going to say, Detective," Steve promised Conrad in a hurried voice. "I don't know why no one has given me the order yet."

Conrad grabbed a metal chair and slid it up to the workstation Steve was sitting at. "Can you locate the signal?"

"I can," Steve assured Conrad and then gave the man a worried eye. "But I haven't been given the order." Steve bit down on his lip. "Detective, something fishy is going on," he continued. "Detective Wallace usually sticks close to this van like a fly on glue…but not today. As a matter of fact, I haven't been getting any communication from the guy."

"I know why," Conrad stated.

"I have a bad feeling I do, too," Steve added. He shook his head and then focused back on a gray metal box that had a bunch of confusing switches, dials, and wires attached to it. "These studios…corrupt," he whispered in a disgusted voice. "In Los Angeles cops get to be cops when dealing with the public—but turn into security guards when it comes to the rich and famous. Sometimes it's enough to make a guy sick, you know?"

"Money turns our badges into tin toys," Conrad agreed, grateful to hear a good cop showing his disgust for the system. "Right now, we need to focus on—"

"Locating the signals…sure." Steve nodded. "When I heard Detective Garland…I mean, Spencer…I mean…your wife…say the word 'beep,' I immediately understood." Steve reached out his right hand and tapped the metal box just as a clap of thunder erupted. The thunder startled Steve, making him jump. "Whew, thought lightning got me for a second."

"Me, too," Conrad said, patting Steve on his shoulder and focusing on the metal box. "Okay, we're looking for…?"

"A deep signal," Steve told Conrad. "I did some research and found out that tons of concrete is sitting under our feet… and under the concrete, tons of dirt." Steve nodded his eyes at the metal box. "I created this little baby myself. Think of it like a radar…sonar…type device."

Conrad studied the metal box with careful eyes. "All right, I will."

"Good," Steve continued. "Now. See that screen that looks like a bunch of squiggles?" Conrad nodded. "That screen is showing me how many people are using their cell phones at this very second. Now look at that screen. See the little dots?" Conrad nodded again. "Hundreds of little dots…representing different locations." Steve tapped a third screen. "This screen shows me the exact location of your wife…see that dot?" Conrad studied the screen and nodded. "I have the depth level set at ground level. But…watch this." Steve reached out and began fiddling with a bunch of knobs and dials. All the screens on the metal box turned blue for a few seconds.

"What are you doing?" Conrad asked.

"Wait and watch," Steve replied. "I haven't tried to go underground yet. We're making the maiden voyage together." Steve continued to fiddle with the dials and knobs for a few more minutes. "I can't find anything," he said, sounding upset. "All I'm getting is silence."

"We might have to wait until Sarah gets another call?" Conrad suggested.

"Maybe," Steve agreed and then added in a concerned voice: "Or maybe my machine can't get through all that concrete and dirt."

Conrad looked at Steve with worried eyes. "Yeah?"

"Hey, I'm not Isaac Newton and—"

"Cool it," Conrad ordered Steve. "Nobody expects more out of you than you can give, okay? All a cop can do is his best, and that's enough."

"Tell that to my boss," Steve said wryly. "In Los Angeles a cop can give his life, but…it doesn't matter." Steve focused back on his invention. "I…"

"Hold up," Conrad called out, staring at the computer

screen. "Sarah's going for her phone…this may be our chance." Steve stiffened and prepared to locate a signal.

"Yes?" Sarah said, answering the call.

"It's time," Patrick announced. "I want to focus on Mr. Earton and Jose Garcia first," he explained and carefully released sensitive details to Sarah that would make any cop dance on a roof. "What is the view count?"

Sarah glanced at the tablet. "Still over ten million."

"Then get to work," Patrick ordered, ending the call and focusing on Ryan. "And you," he added, "it's time you tell me who ran me off the road!"

Ryan stared at Patrick with terrified eyes. "Please—"

"Please nothing," Patrick hissed. He reached into the top desk drawer and pulled out a jar holding a scorpion. "You can either talk to me, boy, or we're going to see how hungry this scorpion is."

Ryan locked his eyes on the jar and saw a large, cruel, angry scorpion trying to escape. Then…he wet his pants. "It wasn't me, Mr. Earton…I swear!"

"Then who?" Patrick demanded, slowly taking the lid off the jar.

Ryan tried to get up and run, but Patrick quickly grabbed his gun and fired a warning shot up at the ceiling. "Sit down!" Ryan began to whimper and beg for his life. "Sit down!"

"Okay…okay…" Ryan slowly sat back down and began begging for his life again. "Mr. Earton…please…I didn't—"

"You went to my brother, didn't you, boy?" Patrick insisted.

"No…no…it was…" Ryan bowed his head in shame. "It was…Patty. But I swear…Patty didn't want to betray you."

"Jill Nayforth?" Patrick asked, holding up the jar holding

the scorpion and dangling it in front of Ryan's face. "Talk or I'm going to feed you to my friend."

Ryan squeezed his eyes closed. "Jill found out Patty was running drugs for you. I don't know how, honest. Patty didn't tell her…Patty doesn't even know Jill found out. There's too many eyes around here." Ryan made a pained face. "Mr. Earton had a meeting with Patty…he threatened to kill her. Patty came to me in tears. She didn't know I was running drugs for you. I made it seem like I was working illegal aliens to save money. Maybe Patty knew? I don't know."

"What did Patty do?" Patrick demanded.

Ryan slowly opened his eyes and saw the hungry scorpion staring at him with cold, deadly eyes. "Nothing," he promised in a shaky voice. "What could Patty do? You had her in a tight spot and so did Mr. Earton."

"Someone ran me off the road," Patrick yelled and struck his desk with a vicious left fist that made the scorpion become agitated. "Don't lie to me!"

"I'm not," Ryan pleaded. "The night you were run off the road, Patty was with me, having dinner at my mother's house. I swear that's the truth. You can call my mother and ask. She hates Patty and wouldn't bother to protect her."

Patrick studied Ryan's eyes. Unfortunately—as far as Patrick could tell—Ryan was telling the truth. "Patty wouldn't have the guts," he said in a low growl. He put the scorpion jar down and began tapping his desk. "It must have been Jill Nayforth…she betrayed me."

"It must have been," Ryan stated, relieved that the scorpion was temporarily shelved. "Mr. Earton—"

Patrick held up his hand. "I will let you and Patty live," he lied. "I need you two to be part of my new operation. In the meantime, shut up and let me think."

Patrick focused back on the computer screen attached to the office wall and watched Sarah begin releasing information that was going to cause his brother to go into a fit of rage and a deadly criminal locked up in a prison in Mexico to follow suit. What Patrick didn't know was that far above his head, Steve was working diligently to locate his position.

"Well?" Conrad asked.

Steve turned in his chair and grinned. "Maybe I'm not so lame after all," he said and tapped a little square screen. "I had my baby set to the wrong depth level. Look at this…" Steve proudly tapped a second screen. "I'm picking up voice waves…and I located the source of the cell phone…both locations match."

Conrad studied the screens as his heart began to race. "Make those lines and dots make sense to me," he told Steve.

"Gladly." Steve beamed and attempted to explain the scene in layman's terms. "In other words, the location of the underground signals are directly under the main building."

"Mr. Earton's office?"

"Bingo." Steve nodded. "Which means—"

"There has to be a tunnel…or an entrance of some kind."

"Yep," Steve agreed. "Our eyes are on the back lot—"

"Looking in the wrong direction!" Conrad grabbed Steve and shook the man's hand. "If you ever want a job in a little snowy Alaskan town, just let me know!" Conrad took off out of the van and started toward the main building on urgent legs. He ran directly into Pete. "Pete, I've located—"

Pete grabbed Conrad's arm and pulled the man to his old car and shoved him inside. "Wallace has ordered me to boot you out of here," he said in a gruff voice. "After I got off the phone with Amanda—"

"Amanda?" Conrad asked, feeling confusion strike his mind.

"I'll explain later," Pete told Conrad. He studied the man's face and then went for a cigar. "What do you have?"

"Steve and I located our hidden rat."

Pete rubbed his chin. "That boy deserves a medal," he said. "Where is the location?"

"Right under the main building."

"Earton's office," Pete grumbled. "I should have known."

Conrad read Pete's face. "What have you got?"

"Besides Wallace protecting Earton?" Pete fussed. Conrad nodded. "Amanda told me, in her own way, she doesn't believe the hidden rat we're looking for has a bomb switch."

"How can Amanda be so certain?" Conrad asked.

"I don't know," Pete answered, chewing on his cigar. He then studied the storm. "Conrad, I've come to realize that our little friend from London would make a good cop."

"Yeah, Amanda is pretty sharp—and she's sure saved my butt a time or two," Conrad agreed.

Pete grew silent for a few seconds. "In other words, we should trust her?" he asked.

"You tell me."

Pete looked over at Conrad and then tapped a closed laptop sitting on the dashboard. "Wallace wants you off the scene…let's see why."

Conrad grabbed the laptop, opened it, and tuned it to Sarah's show. It took no less than five minutes for his mind to understand why Detective Wallace had ordered Pete to get rid of him. "Man," he whistled.

Pete slowly folded his arms. "So that's why Wallace ordered me away from Earton's office and added extra security," he told Conrad in a sick voice.

Conrad glanced over at Pete. "Pete, I have to get into the main building and find my way underground."

"Yes, you do…but not dressed like a New York cop," Pete agreed. "Come on."

"Where?"

"You'll see." Pete hurried out into the storm and led Conrad to a closed studio that was being used to shoot a cop show that most viewers considered a rip-off of *Dragnet*. The back studio door wasn't being guarded, which allowed Pete the time he needed to pick a flimsy lock. "Inside," he ordered. Conrad tossed Pete a confused look and then stepped into a dimly lit hallway lined with closed doors. Pete grabbed Conrad's arm, ran him down the hallway, and then slid to a stop in front of a door that read "Costumes." "Let's make you look like you work for the LAPD." Conrad grinned and stepped into the costume room. Twenty minutes later, he stepped back out into the hallway looking like John from the old television show *CHIPs*. "Ready?"

"Ready," Conrad said.

Pete glanced up and down the hallway and then rubbed his chin. "Conrad?"

"Yeah?"

"I think maybe after we save our girl…I might retire," Pete told Conrad in a tired voice. "The world is changing, and I can't keep up anymore. The private detective business Sarah and I opened…the cases people bring to me…it's not like the old days." Pete kept looking up and down the dim hallway. "Last week I had a nineteen-year-old girl try to hire me to follow her boyfriend around because she thought the guy was stealing her drugs. Can you believe that?"

"In today's world, I can," Conrad told Pete in a voice that sounded exhausted. "The world is growing worse by the day, Pete. Families are falling apart...divorce is rampant...morals... what morals? Kids today are being raised by television, movies, music, video games, computers...smartphones. Parents are nearly obsolete."

"I know," Pete said in a heavy voice. "And cops...except for a rare few...are nothing more than thugs and criminals wearing badges." Pete tossed a hard thumb toward Mr. Earton's office. "Wallace is out there guarding a killer...LA's finest."

Conrad grew silent for a minute and listened to the silence as the smell of old dusty television shows filled his nose. "I liked the show *CHIPs*."

"What?"

"You know...the old show *CHIPs*?"

"Oh...yeah...I think Robert Pines played on that show."

Conrad rolled his eyes. Only Pete would name off a supporting character instead of the two main characters. "When I was a teenager, that show was one of my favorites. You want to know why?"

"Why?"

"Because that show made cops out to be the heroes," Conrad told Pete and patted his friend's shoulder. "We may be few...but we're still heroes. And right now, my wife needs us. We'll worry about the world later."

Pete looked deeply into Conrad's eyes. "You said it." He smiled. "Now all we have to do is figure out a way to get into Earton's office building. Wallace kicked me out and gave strict orders for me to stay out. All the guys guarding the building know my face…" Pete looked up and down the hallway again. "Two guys are guarding the back door. Looks like we're going to have to knock them into dreamland."

"Then let's move," Conrad said. He checked his gun and then rushed back out into the rain with Pete on his tail. Ten minutes later, he crept around to the backside of the three-story building caked with shadows and rain and, for the first time in his life, attacked two cops. That's what a worried husband did when the lives of his wife and unborn child were in danger.

Chapter Fourteen

Sarah, unaware that her husband and old partner had broken the law and officially become criminals, ended the script Patrick had given her to act out and waited for a phone call. And, right on time, her cell phone rang.

"What now?" she asked, answering the call in a cold voice.

"Break time," Patrick informed Sarah. "While we're on break, I want you to send Jill Nayforth backstage. We're going to swap prisoners."

"Swap prisoners?"

Patrick glared up at the bottom of the trap door connected to the backstage. "Yes, swap prisoners. I want to speak with Jill Nayforth. Is that clear?"

Patrick's voice sounded different to Sarah. Well, not so much his voice but how his voice seemed more…open… rather than closed in. *He's changed location,* Sarah thought to herself and carefully glanced toward backstage. "I need to see…" Sarah quickly waved for Amanda to join her in front of the tablet. Amanda jumped up from a chair and hauled butt over to Sarah. "Call your hubby," Sarah whispered in Amanda's ear and nodded at the tablet. "I need to see if our hidden enemy is watching us."

Amanda studied Sarah's eyes and then did as asked. "Why do you want to swap prisoners?" Sarah asked as Amanda made her call.

"Do as I say or I'll detonate the bombs," Patrick warned Sarah.

Sarah wasn't so certain Patrick could fulfill his promise but wasn't willing to take the chance. Amanda was confident that the monster was faking and had informed Pete of her theory but had yet to tell Sarah. Being right was one thing; being wrong meant losing it all. Pete would have to think of a plan to save everyone while Amanda and Sarah played nice with the hidden creature under the stage. Or so Amanda hoped and prayed. "Will you?" Sarah asked, pretending to sound uncertain yet a tad stubborn.

Patrick detested the fact that Sarah had located the bomb switch and that he wasn't in possession of a bomb switch himself. Bluffing a cop was proving to be a tedious chore. "Is your unborn child worth finding out?"

"No," Sarah answered. She looked at Jill and sighed. "Promise you will not harm Jill?"

"I'm simply after answers…at the moment," Patrick explained, keeping his eyes peeled on the bottom of the trap door while keeping a gun pointed straight at Ryan. Behind him stood a long, dark, damp tunnel filled with eerie sounds and creepy shadows lurking about. "I have more work for you to do, Detective."

Sarah focused back on Amanda. Amanda was speaking to her husband in a low whisper with gentle tears falling from her eyes. It was clear that the unknown man wasn't watching the live stream, which allowed Sarah to take the game up a notch. It was time to confirm who the creature hiding under the stage was.

"I hope you're right, honey," she whispered. She cleared her throat and then asked: "Am I talking to Patrick Earton?"

Patrick felt anger enter his eyes but quickly caught hold of his temper. "How did you arrive at that conclusion?"

"My husband did," Sarah stated in a proud voice. "Surely you realize that I have a team working on the outside."

"Yes," Patrick said. "So be it, Detective. The world is going to learn the truth by the time we end this little game anyway. Now, bring me Jill Nayforth or Ryan Mables eats a bullet."

"So be it," Sarah told Patrick. "Give me five minutes. I don't think the woman is going to cooperate on her own free will."

"Five minutes or Ryan Mables is dead," Patrick warned.

Sarah quickly ended her call and then dialed Conrad's cell phone. "Honey, Patrick Earton is under the backstage and—"

"Pete and I are in a basement under the main building searching for a tunnel," Conrad informed Sarah in a careful voice as he eased past a mountain of machines that were clattering and fussing. "We've located Patrick Earton."

Sarah felt her heart jump. "Patrick Earton isn't watching the live stream…" Sarah bit down on her lip as Amanda ended her call. "He wants to switch Ryan with Jill Nayforth…I don't have a choice," she whispered.

"Do as you're told," Conrad pleaded, using a small penlight to find his way through the creepy basement that seemed large enough to swallow an entire city block. "Pete… any ideas?"

Pete shook his head. "No," he said, slicing through the

darkness with his own penlight. "But we better hurry because when those two boys we knocked cold and dragged in here don't answer their roll call, we're going to be in deep water."

"Sarah, honey, just do as Patrick Earton demands—for now, at least. Once Pete and I find our way in, we'll handle the guy," Conrad promised.

"Okay," Sarah whispered. "Please…just be careful," she begged.

"Hey, we have a baby that's going to need a mommy and a daddy," Conrad told Sarah. He forced a weak smile to his face and continued. "But from now on, what do you say we just stay home and watch my old black-and-white movies?"

Sarah looked over at Amanda, saw her best friend wipe a few tears out of her eyes, and sighed. "I think Amanda would agree with that. I love you, honey…please be careful."

"Will do." Conrad reluctantly ended the call and looked at Pete. "This is like trying to find a needle in a—"

"Don't say it," Pete fussed. He aimed the penlight in his hand at the north end of the basement. "I'll check the north end…you check the south. Hurry."

Conrad nodded and jogged off into the darkness, leaving Pete to wander alone to the north end. "Stupid basement," Pete fussed under his breath, walking past low-hanging pipes that appeared rusted and out of service. Newer, modern pipes were hanging next to the rusted pipes, as if they were boasting of their purpose. Pete reached up and touched one of the newer pipes and then slid his hand over to a rusted pipe. As he did, an idea struck his mind.

"I wonder…" Pete quickly took an old pocketknife out of the pocket of his overcoat, opened it, and began digging into the rusted pipe. The pipe, to Pete's relief, was so old and rusted that the blade cut through in less than a minute, creating a small hole.

"Air," Pete said, sticking his left hand over the small hole and feeling air escaping. "Cold air…" Pete quickly followed the rusted pipe to the far north basement wall. The pipe took a quick dive underground. Pete looked behind a pile of old, rusted metal filing cabinets. He whistled for Conrad and then pushed his way behind the filing cabinets and studied a damp concrete floor. At first, all his old eyes consumed was a damp concrete floor…but then the beam on the penlight flashed over what appeared to be a little keyhole dug into the floor. Pete dropped down onto his knees and examined the keyhole that was friends with a lock that had been stationed in the floor.

"What is it?" Conrad asked, arriving to find Pete on his knees, studying something on the floor.

"A keyhole…and a lock," Pete explained. "I think we've located our entry…just give me a second to pick the lock." Pete put his pocketknife away and retrieved a lockpicking device. "Never leave home without one of these goodies," he told Conrad.

Conrad grinned. "I'll remember that the next time I go on vacation."

Pete grinned back and then went to work on the lock. A minute later, a metallic *click* filled the basement air. "We're in business," Pete whispered as a hidden door attached to the basement floor popped open just enough for someone to be able to open it.

Conrad yanked out his gun. "Get Steve on the phone. We're going to need him to be our eyes."

"Yep," Pete agreed, whipping out his cell phone and calling Steve. "Guide our path, son."

Steve tensed up. "You found a way down?"

"We sure have."

Steve glanced over his shoulder in order to make sure no one was watching him. "It's getting chaotic, Pete," he stated. "After Detective Garland's…I mean, Spencer's…last broadcast…well, I got a call to exit the studio grounds. A lot of our guys are being told to take a hike. What in the world is going on?"

"Power and money," Pete told Steve as he watched Conrad ease open the hidden door. "My guess is Earton called the mayor's office."

"Yeah, that's what Zach told me a few minutes ago," Steve agreed. "Rumor is the mayor is due to arrive at any minute." Steve shook his head. "The strange thing is, the bomb squad has been told to take a hike, too."

"Really?" Pete asked in a concerned voice.

"Yeah," Steve confirmed. "Zach told me some of our guys out on patrol saw the mayor's limousine being followed by three black vans?" Steve checked over his shoulder again. "I don't like this, Pete. Something is up."

"You're telling me," Pete agreed and continued to chew on his cigar. "Okay, son, stand tight and be our eyes. Conrad and I are going underground. I'll leave my cell phone on speakerphone…you just guide us in the right direction."

Steve shifted in his chair. "Pete, I'm supposed to be moving out."

"Get out of the van and flatten one of the tires," Pete urged Steve. "No, flatten two of the tires."

"I'll be seen," Steve objected.

"By who?" Pete barked. "A bunch of retreating cops?"

Steve hesitated. "Yeah…okay…I guess you're right. Give me a few minutes."

"We'll be going below," Pete told Steve and then looked at Conrad. "What do you see?"

"Steel ladder rings attached to the wall. We can climb down," Conrad told Pete. He shoved the penlight into his mouth, put his gun away, and then began a dangerous and unknown descent into a dark hole filled with a history of misery, murder, terror, and darkness. Pete, who hated tight spaces, rubbed his eyes, put his cell phone under his chin, shoved the penlight he was holding into his mouth, and followed after Conrad.

As Pete climbed down into a deep tunnel, Sarah approached Jill. "We have to make a switch," she explained. "A man named Patrick Earton wants to speak with you…but I assume you already knew the man's name?"

Jill's eyes grew wide with shock. How did Sarah find out Patrick's name? "I…no…it's…"

"Jill, you can surrender all the answers I need later. Right now, unless you do as told, Patrick Earton will kill Ryan."

"Do as you're told!" Patty snapped at Jill.

"You shut up," Sarah fired at Patty. "I'm growing very tired of you, Patty. My patience with you has reached an end."

"Oh, go shove it—" Patty began to scream at Sarah but was stopped mid-sentence by a hard fist that knocked her out cold.

"Ouch…that hurt," Amanda cried out and began rubbing her right fist. "Oh…that's going to bruise…ouch…" She began turning in little circles. "Oh, that fussy little pigeon… oh…"

Sarah felt a grin touch her lips. Amanda sure was something. "June Bug—"

"Not now, love...I think I broke something," Amanda whined as she continued to dance around.

Sarah quickly checked Amanda's hand. Gratefully, not a single bone was broken. "I think you're going to live, June Bug."

Amanda made a pained face, threw her eyes at Jill, and then pulled Sarah off to the side. "Love, I wasn't going to tell you this, but...well, I called Pete after you talked to Conrad... and I told him that I don't believe that this Patrick Earton bloke has a bomb switch. I'm only telling you this now because I'm afraid if we give Jill over...she'll meet her end."

"What reason do you have for your theory?" Sarah asked Amanda in a quick voice.

"I guess there could be more than one bomb switch...but I've been thinking..." Amanda turned her back to the tablet. "If there are two bomb switches, why is our little slimy sewer rat staying underground? Surely, love, he could emerge and hide someplace in this studio, right? I mean, call me stupid, but it seems to me the rat is staying far away from the bombs."

"We do have a bomb switch ourselves," Sarah pointed out. "Of course we aren't about to blow ourselves up and—"

Amanda walked her eyes over to Jill. "Love, you didn't let me finish," she whispered. "Everything I told you makes me think our rat is bluffing...but what cinches the apple in the pie is that woman." Amanda nodded at Jill. "The little fussy pigeon I just put to sleep has been on edge, but Jill...her nervousness is edgy. I can't really put a finger on it. Jill just doesn't seem to be worried about being blown to smithereens."

Sarah studied Jill, who was staring at her with scared eyes.

And then, to Sarah's horror, the woman threw her eyes around and then took off running. "Jill!" Sarah cried out. "Jill…stop!"

"Told you," Amanda yelled as Sarah grabbed her arm and they took off running after Jill.

Sarah quickly took out her gun and fired three warning shots into the air as Jill reached backstage and began aiming for the exit door. "We don't know where the bombs are. If we open any of the doors, the bombs could go off!" she hollered at Jill. "Get away from the door…now!"

Jill turned on Sarah. "I'm not going to let Patrick Earton kill me…do you hear me? I'm the killer that deranged clown was after! I ran Patrick Earton off the road…I tried to kill him! If you let that man get his hands on me, I'm dead!"

Sarah glanced at the hidden trap door. Even if Amanda was right about Patrick bluffing, Sarah had no idea where the three bombs were hidden. Could opening a door set off the bombs? Sarah didn't know. All she knew was that the so-called relaxing game show she had agreed to be a guest on had become intense and filled with sharp pieces of broken glass. "Hold on, baby," Sarah whispered to her baby and gently rubbed her tender belly with her left hand. "Mommy is going to figure out how to get us out of this nightmare in one piece."

"Uh…love," Amanda whispered and threw a finger at the hidden trap door. Sarah looked down, saw the trap door open just enough to allow a gun barrel to appear, and then grabbed Amanda and hit the floor just as a bullet erupted in the air and went flying over her head.

Chapter Fifteen

Pete spotted the rusted pipe he had cut a small hole in while standing in the basement. The pipe ended halfway down the hole he was climbing down into. A large hole had formed on the bottom of the pipe, the rust completely eating through the rest of the metal. Pete stuck out his left hand, felt the pipe, and then continued to descend into the dark hole.

"Easy now," Conrad called up to Pete, standing on the damp concrete floor. Pete nodded and managed to reach the bottom of the hole. Conrad carefully helped him secure confident footing and then pointed down a long tunnel that was lit with what appeared to be mini torch lights. "Ready?" he asked Pete, pulling out his gun.

"Ready," Pete confirmed. "I'll cover our rear...you take lead point."

"Let's move." Conrad put away his penlight, placed his gun at the ready, and began moving down a long, narrow tunnel that felt like the mouth of a deranged clown. Pete glanced up at the hole he had climbed down, shook his head, and began following Conrad.

As Conrad and Pete cautiously moved further into the darkness, Sarah heard a second gunshot…and then she heard Jill cry out in pain. With no time to think, she rolled over onto her right side and fired three shots at the trap door. The bullets forced Patrick to retreat.

"Jill!" Sarah called out and spun her head around. Jill was lying on the floor holding her left shoulder. "Amanda?"

"Right here, love," Amanda yelled.

Sarah looked around and saw Amanda crawl out from behind the stage curtain. Relief washed through her heart. "You're okay…she's okay," Sarah whispered as tears began to fall from her eyes. She struggled to her feet, ran to Amanda, and embraced her friend. "You're okay!"

Amanda hugged Sarah back. "Crazy bloke shot at us," she said, feeling her own tears appear, and then pointed at Jill. "She's hurt."

Sarah nodded and ran over to Jill. Jill tried to wiggle away, but Sarah grabbed her left leg. "Let me see how bad you're hurt, Jill," she demanded. Jill looked up into Sarah's fierce eyes, saw a caring woman—and maybe even a friend—and caved. Sarah quickly checked Jill's left shoulder. "Bullet grazed your shoulder…no full impact," she stated in a relieved voice.

Amanda locked her eyes on the hidden trap door. The door was closed. "Think you hit him?" she asked in a hopeful voice.

Sarah stood up and studied the trap door. "One thing is for certain…if Patrick Earton does have a second bomb switch, we're soon to find out—and I don't want to wait around." Sarah turned to Jill. "Honey, please, if there is another way out of here—"

"There is," Jill promised Sarah. "Please help me stand up." Amanda quickly took Jill's right hand and helped the woman stand. "Listen to me. I know what you must be thinking…and you're right. I'm a horrible person, but it's not what you think. I was pushed into a corner. I…wasn't given a choice."

"Jill, honey, later," Sarah pleaded. "Right now, we need a way out of here. We can't use the main entry and exit doors."

"The bombs," Amanda reminded Jill. "If we open any of the doors, we could risk…well…boom!"

"There is one other way out," Jill explained, becoming so shaky she nearly collapsed. "Oh my…all this stress…" She placed her left hand over her forehead like a fainting actress.

"No time for that, sis," Amanda told Jill and quickly slapped the woman across her face. Sarah winced and waited for Jill to either faint or retaliate. To her relief, Jill simply stared at Amanda with shocked eyes and then managed to stop shaking. "Better?" Amanda asked.

"Better," Jill said. She took a second to clear her mind and then pointed up. "There's a fire escape in the maintenance room. The maintenance room is located at the back of the studio. It's a crummy room that's hard to find…more like a broom closet filled with old tools."

Amanda looked at Sarah with hopeful eyes. "Love?"

Sarah nodded. "Conrad and Pete found a way into the underground tunnels," she explained and pointed at the trap door. "Take Jill and get out of here, June Bug. I'm going to get Patty and—" Before Sarah could say another word, the trap door began to open again. Sarah dropped down onto one knee and prepared to fire.

"Don't shoot…it's me…it's Ryan!" Ryan called out in a miserable voice.

Sarah watched Ryan ease the trap door open. His head appeared and then his upper body. "Where is Patrick Earton?" Sarah demanded, aiming her gun at the trap door.

"Hurt," Ryan called out as he struggled out of the trap door, using his handcuffed hands to pull his body out. "He's shot."

Sarah, seeing that Ryan's hands were handcuffed, stood up, worked her way to the guy, and moved him to Jill's position. "How did you escape?"

Ryan licked his lips. Patrick had ordered him to deceive Sarah or else Patty would die. It was now or never. But as Ryan looked into Sarah's eyes, he saw a kind woman who was pregnant—an innocent woman who simply wanted to be a mommy. Sarah wasn't the bad guy. Sarah was a decent woman who took risks to save innocent lives. Patrick Earton was the bad guy…and, Ryan miserably thought, so was he. Yes, it was now or never…it was time to either lose his heart or renew his integrity and courage. "I may lose Patty…but I will never be able to live with myself," he whispered.

"What?" Amanda asked. "Speak up, you creepy bloke!"

"I said I would never be able to live with myself," Ryan stated in a clear voice and then looked at Jill. "Looks like Patrick caught us all in his spider web, huh?" he said.

"I'm afraid so," Jill confessed.

"You ran Patrick Earton off the road, didn't you?" Ryan asked. Jill nodded. "You were the killer those crazy clowns were after?" Jill nodded again. "Well…Patty and I aren't innocent…we were running drugs for Patrick. I guess it's time to man up and take responsibility."

"Where is Patrick Earton?" Sarah demanded.

"Hurt," Ryan honestly answered. "When he tried to shoot Jill…I guess you were the one who shot back at him?"

"Yes," Sarah confirmed.

Ryan nodded at the trap door. "You got Patrick in his hand…his left hand, I think? He ordered me to come up here and tell you that he's laying down there dead. He's planning to ambush you."

"Does Patrick Earton have a bomb switch?" Sarah asked Ryan in an urgent voice.

"I don't know. I mean, he never mentioned anything to me…" Ryan closed his eyes and tried to think. "I didn't see any bomb switch when I was in that office…I…mean…I don't know?"

"What office?" Sarah demanded.

"Some old office that Patrick took me to," Ryan explained. He opened his eyes, looked around, and asked where Patty was.

"Out cold," Amanda stated and tossed a thumb toward the front stage.

Ryan began to run toward the front stage, but Sarah grabbed his arm. "I told you all I know!" he insisted. "Please, I have to get to Patty—"

"You're going to show me where that office is," Sarah told Ryan.

"Are you crazy? Patrick Earton is waiting below…he'll kill us. I have to get Patty out of here and—"

"You're going to help me," Sarah ordered Ryan, pushing him over to Amanda. She called Conrad's cell phone. "Please let the signal reach him," she whispered and waited as static filled her ears. And then, just when it seemed that the call wasn't going to be a success, Conrad answered. "Conrad?"

"Sarah?" Conrad called out as he neared the end of the long tunnel he and Pete were walking down. "I can barely hear you—"

"Patrick Earton is hurt. He might be under the main stage, or he could be moving back in your direction." Sarah looked at Ryan. Could the guy be trusted? She wasn't certain. It appeared that Ryan was finally using his brains, but a good cop always used caution. "There's an office...can you hear me?"

"Barely...keep talking!" Conrad yelled into his cell phone.

"There's an office—I'm going to have Ryan Mables show me where the office is!"

"No...Patrick Earton is waiting below!" Ryan insisted.

Sarah studied Ryan's panicked eyes. Okay, she decided, the guy was telling the truth. "Find the office, Conrad...I'm going to smoke Patrick Earton back in your direction!"

"What...smoke?" Conrad asked, but there was silence. "Lost the call," he said to Pete.

"What did our gal say?" Pete asked, taking a second to catch his breath. "I feel like a trapped rat down here..."

Conrad glanced down the tunnel and then focused his eyes on a wooden door that was attached to a wall waiting at the end of the tunnel. "Patrick Earton is hurt...something about an office...and smoke?"

Pete thought for a second. "Patrick Earton is hurt... something about an office?" he finally spoke and looked at Conrad. "Sarah is going to try and smoke Earton back in our direction. We need to move."

"Hold on." Conrad tried to call Sarah. The call failed. "Stupid phone!"

"Look," Pete told Conrad in a stern tone, "I know my gal…I know her codes. We need to get moving."

Conrad nodded and hurried to the wooden door. "Another lock."

"Not a problem," Pete promised. He quickly retrieved his lockpicking device, picked the lock, and stepped back from the wooden door. "I'll cover you."

Conrad studied the wooden door and then drew in a deep breath. "Let's move," he said and used his left hand to turn a rusted knob. He waited until the door opened up a few inches, then kicked it open and burst into another tunnel with his gun at the ready. Pete stormed into the new tunnel right behind Conrad. "Clear!" Conrad said.

"Maybe not," Pete said and pointed to his right. A closed fancy office door appeared in Conrad's sight. "And look at this," Pete continued. He lowered his gun and pointed up at the top of the wooden door Conrad had kicked open. "See those wires…"

"I see them," Conrad said in a miserable voice. "I just set off an alarm."

"Yeah…but let's see if Patrick Earton is home to notice the alarm. Ready?"

"Ready!" Conrad said. He moved to the fancy office door, waited for Pete to get into position, and then used his right foot to kick the door open. "Hands in the air!" Conrad screamed as he charged into Patrick's hidden office. Unfortunately, Patrick Earton wasn't home. "Clear!"

Pete rushed into the office and studied the interior. "Try our girl again…hurry."

"My cell phone—"

"Earton was making calls from this office," Pete insisted. "Look!" Pete pointed to the computer screen attached to the office wall. "That's a live view of the main stage. He's been watching Sarah this entire time…which means he's been able to put calls through."

"Okay…I'll try." Conrad lowered his gun, whipped his cell phone out, and called Sarah. To his relief, a clear call went through. "Sarah…we're in the office. Patrick Earton isn't around."

"Patrick Earton is under the stage," Sarah told Conrad, nearly bursting into tears. "Oh, you and Pete…I owe you two the biggest kisses, honey. I was…so scared we might—"

"Don't say it," Conrad begged, fighting back his own tears. "Listen, Pete and I are moving in your direction. If you can secure the trap door—"

"I'm going to smoke Patrick Earton back in your direction," Sarah promised.

"No!" Conrad begged. "Sarah, let me and Pete flush out the rat and—" Before Conrad could finish, a shadowy figure appeared in the office doorway out of nowhere and stuck a gun to Pete's head.

"Drop the call and your gun," Richie Stevens ordered Conrad. "Or he's dead."

Conrad stared into the face of a man who meant business. He dropped the cell phone, deliberately leaving it on, and then placed his gun down onto Patrick's desk. "Okay…take it easy."

Richie ordered Pete to drop his gun. Pete did as ordered. "Get over there," he snapped, shoving Pete toward Conrad. He then pulled a cell phone out of the pocket of the black leather jacket he was wearing and called Patrick. "I've caught two intruders."

Patrick, standing in a connector tunnel waiting for Sarah to appear, grimaced in pain. "She shot up my left hand," he hissed under his breath, struggling to hold the gun in his right hand steady. "Who are the intruders?"

"Who are you?" Richie demanded, glaring at Conrad and Pete. "No lies!"

"Your worst nightmare, punk," Pete snapped.

"Cut out the heroics," Richie fired at Pete. "Don't make me cut you down!"

Pete glanced at the scorpion jar sitting on Patrick's desk. Richie was standing just close enough for Pete to launch the jar like a rocket. And thanks to Patrick Earton, the lid on the jar wasn't secure.

"What are you doing, you ugly…ugly…punk…" Pete stopped talking and grabbed his chest with his left hand. "Oh…not now…not this way!" he called out and crashed down onto the desk, deliberately knocking the scorpion jar over and pulling it under his chest.

"Hey…what's with him!" Richie demanded. "Mr. Earton…call you back." Richie ended the call and stared at Pete. "What's with the old man?"

"He's having a heart attack!" Conrad yelled, uncertain what Pete was up to but determined to trust the man. "We need to get him out of here!"

"Hey…old man…get up!" Richie ordered and then, feeling confident that the Glock 19 he was holding would keep his two captives beaten down, he took a few steps toward the desk. "Hey, old man…get up!"

"My…chest," Pete whimpered. "Call…an ambulance…"

"I said get up!" Richie yelled, pointing his gun at Conrad. He grabbed Pete by his coat collar.

"Gladly!" Pete yelled. He jerked his body up and slung a very vicious and angry scorpion at Richie's face. Richie saw the scorpion flying in the air, stumbled backward, tripped over his feet, and hit the floor. The scorpion landed right on his chest. Pete didn't waste a second. He spun around and kicked the gun Richie was holding into the air.

"Hey, man…get…get this thing off me…please," Richie begged, staring at the scorpion that was now perched on his chest in an attack position.

Conrad grinned. Good ol' Pete. "Hang on, Pete," he said. He retrieved his gun and then went for the cell phone. "We're okay, honey…Pete just caught a shadow."

"Who is he?" Sarah asked.

"What's your name?" Conrad asked Richie. "The truth or I'm going to kick that scorpion in your face."

"Richie…Richie Stevens," Richie cried out. "Please…get this thing off me."

"Richie Stevens?" Sarah whispered and looked toward the main stage. Patty was still out cold. Amanda had really slugged the girl. "Okay, Conrad, it's time to end this game show. I'm going to smoke Patrick Earton back to you…my way."

"What's your plan?" Conrad asked.

"Just be prepared for a visitor," Sarah told her husband and checked her gun. "I'm going for the main prize."

Chapter Sixteen

"Jill," Sarah said, "get out of here. Ryan, go get Patty and…never cross my eyesight again. Is that clear?"

"Sarah?" Jill asked in a shocked voice. "I don't understand. You're a cop—"

"I'm a retired cop," Sarah pointed out. "I'm letting you go because I want you to go to the cops and confess everything…you too, Ryan. But if you run, you'll make your lives worse than they already are." Sarah pointed to the tablet sitting on the front stage. "Over ten million people are watching…well, were watching. That's ten million witnesses to what has taken place here today. You have that on your side."

Jill stared at Sarah and then ran off into the darkness without saying a word. "Thank you," Ryan told Sarah.

"Don't thank me," Sarah replied. "You're not innocent, Ryan. But you do have a chance to change your life. I hope you make the right choice." Sarah pointed to the exit door. "Go through that door. Jill said there's a fire exit in an old maintenance room. Use the fire exit…do not use the main doors. If you do, the bombs might detonate."

"Sure…got it," Ryan promised and held up the handcuffs holding his wrists together. "A little help."

"My husband has captured Richie Stevens," Sarah informed Ryan. "Patty Darling has a lot of answering to do, but it's clear that you two love each other. Ryan," Sarah paused and touched her tummy, "I'm going to have my baby in a few months…and if Patty were my daughter, I would want to give her a second chance. Help her." Sarah pulled out a pair of handcuff keys and freed Ryan. "If you were my son, I would want you to have a second chance. Make it count."

Ryan rubbed his wrists. "I'm not innocent," he sighed. "I let Patrick Earton—"

"Tell the cops your story," Sarah told Ryan and nodded at the front stage. "Now move." Ryan nodded and ran to the front stage, scooped Patty up in his arms, and hurried away.

"Okay, love, what now?" Amanda asked.

"We're going to get ourselves a rat," Sarah explained. She walked over to the trap door and eased it open just enough to allow her voice to flow through. "You don't have a bomb switch, Patrick!" she yelled. "I've sent Patty, Ryan, and Jill outside! I'm leaving with my friend. My husband will be arriving any minute with countless cops. You better run!"

Patrick heard Sarah's words. His face turned red with rage. "You killed my daughter…you're going to suffer! But first…it's Jill Nayforth I want dead! I'll deal with you later!" Patrick promised and began to fall back toward his office, knowing that as soon as Sarah opened any of the main entry or exit doors, the three bombs Sophia and Lyle had set would detonate. Maybe he wouldn't kill Sarah personally…but the bombs would surely take care of the woman. Besides, Sarah had caused enough damage to Patrick's brother and Jose

Garcia to allow Patrick to take full control. So what if his carefully formed plan had fallen apart—the end result was the same, and that's what mattered.

Sarah heard the sound of footsteps echoing under the stage. Patrick was running away. "Okay, honey, I spooked Patrick Earton. He's coming your way."

"Got it!" Conrad handed Richie's cell phone to him. "Make the call."

Richie stared at the scorpion sitting on his chest and carefully called Patrick. "Yeah…it's Richie…I had to gun down the two cops I caught in your office…you better hurry."

"The entire building is about to explode," Patrick told Richie, running through the tunnels. "I'll be to my office in five minutes. Start clearing my desk and the filing cabinet." Patrick ended the call and then slid to a stop. He threw his head back toward the area Sarah was in and narrowed his eyes. "If the building doesn't explode," he hissed, "I'll find you, Jill…and I'll make you suffer, Detective Garland," he promised and then started running again.

"Let's move," Sarah told Amanda. She pulled the trap door open and crawled down into a dark hole. Amanda grimaced, promised to never leave Alaska ever again, and followed after Sarah. At least, she thought, climbing down into the hole, if the building explodes, she and Sarah would be…somewhat… safe.

Sarah checked the cold, dimly lit tunnel sitting under the stage, waited for Amanda, and then broke off into a jog. "Let's hope Ryan gave us the right directions."

"Forget the directions…follow the blood trail." Amanda pointed down at the tunnel floor. Sarah spotted an ugly trail of red and broke off into a cautious jog.

As Sarah started to trail Patrick, Patrick decided to play it smart and enter his office using a secret passageway he had built with his own two hands. No one—not a single living person—knew about the secret passageway. Ducking into a side tunnel, still bleeding from his left hand, Patrick hurried down a short tunnel that dived deeper into the earth. He stopped at a flimsy wooden door, opened it, and stepped into a dark, dirt room. A trap door was stationed on the ceiling of the room. Patrick moved over to a wooden ladder and, using his elbows for support, climbed up the ladder and silently eased open a small trap door that opened up under his desk. Patrick immediately heard voices and spotted Conrad's and Pete's legs standing off to the right side of the desk. He narrowed his eyes, eased up out of the trap door like a slithering shadow, and before Conrad or Pete knew what was happening, he exploded out from under the desk with his gun prepared to fire. "Don't move!"

Conrad threw his eyes at Patrick. Where in the world had the man come from? "Okay…okay…take it easy," he said in a voice that appeared to sound cool.

"Drop your guns! Now!"

Pete carefully dropped his gun. "Do it, Conrad." Conrad hesitated and then dropped his gun.

"Hey…get this thing off me," Richie begged Patrick.

Patrick glanced down, saw his scorpion perched on Richie's chest, and shook his head. "You're in the perfect position," he said and then focused back on Conrad. "You're not as smart as you hoped," he stated, feeling secure in his office. "You're trespassing in territory that is my own." Patrick narrowed his eyes. "Who are you?"

"Conrad Spencer."

"Ah…the husband." Patrick grinned. "You've come to play the part of a hero, I see. But I'm afraid it's too late. Your wife, without knowing it, is going to kill off all of my enemies—including herself. All she has to do is open one of the main exit doors." Patrick checked his watch. "Which should be any second now. Once I hear an explosion, I'm going to kill you."

What Patrick didn't know was that Sarah and Amanda had followed his blood trail straight to the hidden room. "Stay here, June Bug," Sarah whispered and began crawling up the wooden ladder. When she reached the trap door, she eased it open and began listening to Patrick threatening to kill Conrad and Pete. "Time to end this and go home," she whispered, easing out of the trap door. She peeked her head out from under the desk, spotted Patrick, and fired off a clear shot.

The last thing Patrick Earton remembered before joining Sophia Johnson in an eternal darkness was waiting for an explosion to occur, confident that Sarah was foolish enough to open one of the main exit doors. What Patrick Earton didn't understand was that Sarah was an angry, hungry, pregnant woman who was ready to go home.

Sarah quickly crawled out from under the desk, popped her head up, and smiled at Conrad and Pete. "You know… you're the ones who are supposed to be saving me," she said as tears began falling from her eyes. "June Bug, get up here!"

Amanda didn't waste any time. She scrambled up the wooden ladder, crawled out from under Patrick's desk, spotted a dead body and a man lying on the floor with a scorpion sitting on his chest, made a disgusted face, and ran over to Pete. "Hi, handsome, mind if I use your phone to call my hubby?"

Pete laughed, hugged Amanda, and walked her out of the office. "I think those two might need a minute."

Conrad ran to Sarah, swooped her up into his arms, and kissed her all over. "I'm never letting you leave my sight again."

"That works for me," Sarah cried, kissing Conrad back. She placed his hand onto her belly. "Let's go home…and when we get home you can tell me why you're dressed like John from *CHIPs*."

"What about me?" Richie begged.

"Oh yeah…you," Conrad sighed. "I guess I better snatch this punk up."

"All in a day's work," Sarah told Conrad, kissing his cheeks. She then joined Pete and Amanda out in the tunnel while Conrad saved Richie from the scorpion. "Pete," she said in a tired voice, "the next time I decide to go on a game show…slug me."

Pete grinned, reached into his coat pocket, pulled out his half-smoked cigar, and said: "What do you expect, kiddo? This is Los Angeles."

Sarah let out an exhausted laugh.

One week later, Sarah walked through the back door of her cabin in Alaska and ran to Mittens. "Oh, my baby," she said, hugging the happy Husky. Mittens began licking Sarah all over her face.

"Oh, home sweet home," Conrad called out. He dropped an armload of suitcases and stretched his back.

"Hey, you're home," Manford called out and hurried into the kitchen. He ran over to Sarah and hugged her. "Man, can't you go anywhere without getting into trouble?"

Sarah hugged Manford back, kissed his cheeks, and pointed a finger at a very exhausted Amanda who was trailing in behind Conrad. "Blame her."

"Not funny, love," Amanda said, feeling way too tired to fuss. The brown dress she was wearing—a dress that cost a pretty penny and was supposed to be the newest design—was plum ugly and made her look like a piece of driftwood. Her hair was all messy and her tummy was hungry. "All I want to do is sleep."

"Here?" Manford asked.

"My hubby had to fly back to London, you little bloke," Amanda told Manford, dropping two suitcases down onto the kitchen floor. She patted Conrad's shoulder and wandered away toward the spare bedroom. "You sleep on the couch," she told Manford and vanished.

Sarah grinned at Manford. "The couch it is."

"Oh, great," Manford complained and watched Conrad take off his leather jacket. "You married her."

"Yes, I did." Conrad smiled, staring at Sarah and finding the woman beautiful in the soft blue dress she was wearing. "Yes, Manford, I did marry—"

"A good woman."

Conrad spun around and saw Andrew stick his head through the back door. "Oh…it's you," he said in a sour tone.

"Yeah, it's me," Andrew said, dressed in a hunting outfit instead of his chief of police uniform. "I…was told you were back in town. I wanted to stop in and tell you that my wife's friend…well, she spent three days behind bars and was charged with assaulting an officer of the law." Andrew lifted his hand and scratched the back of his neck. "I was…wrong, Conrad, to take sides. I…well, you're a good cop, and my best friend, and well…I guess I better go if I want to get in some good hunting."

Sarah quickly gave Conrad a look. Conrad rolled his eyes and nodded. Even though his mind was exhausted, he knew what needed to be done. "I can get my rifle and join you."

Andrew cheered up. "Does that mean you'll be to work Monday morning?"

Conrad offered his friend a smile. "Lousy coffee…stale donuts…you bet. Let me go use the bathroom and get my hunting jacket and rifle."

Andrew watched Conrad hurry out of the kitchen and then looked at Sarah. "So, how was the game show?" he asked.

Sarah shot Andrew a confused eye. "You mean you don't know?"

"Man, where have you been?" Manford asked Andrew before wandering back into the living room to finish off an old black-and-white movie he had been watching.

"Did I miss something?" Andrew asked Sarah.

Sarah sighed. "Close the kitchen door and I'll explain."

Andrew closed the door, sat down at the kitchen table, and waited for Sarah to tell him how her trip to Los Angeles had been. "Well?"

Sarah patted Andrew's shoulder. "Coffee first…decaf," she said. She made a fresh pot of coffee and pulled a plate of donuts out of the refrigerator and sat down. "Andrew, let me begin by saying there's no place like home."

"Uh…sure, our little town is home," Andrew replied as he studied Sarah's face. "Sarah, what happened in Los Angeles?"

Sarah picked up a plain donut and had just begun to explain about how a game show designed to bring a little fun to pregnant women had turned into a nightmare when

Amanda burst into the kitchen fussing up a storm. "That bloke you call a husband pushed me out of the bathroom!" Amanda threw her hands up into the air, plopped down at the kitchen table, and grabbed Sarah's donut out of her hand. "He told me I look like burnt tree bark." Amanda threw her eyes at Andrew. "Not a word, you miserable bloke!"

Andrew threw his hands up into the air. "I didn't say anything."

"Oh, but you were thinking it. You men…make me sick!" Amanda gobbled down her donut and went for another. "Love, the morning is early. Let's go to O'Mally's and get in some shopping."

"I thought all you wanted was sleep?" Sarah teased.

"Well," Amanda said, gobbling down her second donut, "I may need some kosher chili dogs to help me sleep…and a few new blouses…and some new dresses…"

Sarah grinned. Amanda was one of a kind. "Let's go, June Bug," she said, standing up. She grabbed Amanda's hand and rushed outside, leaving Andrew alone with Mittens.

Andrew looked at Mittens with confused eyes. "Don't ask me, girl." He shrugged his shoulders and waited for Conrad. When Conrad appeared, Andrew stood up, shrugged his shoulders again, and walked outside. One thing was for certain: With Sarah and Amanda in Snow Falls, life was never going to be boring—and O'Mally's department store was never going to be able to keep a fresh stock of kosher chili dogs. That was life, and a good life at that—even if there were still creepy snowmen chewing candy canes and wearing leather jackets lurking about.

About Wendy Meadows

Wendy Meadows, a USA Today bestselling author, delights readers with her engaging stories about women sleuths. She has penned numerous books, including the beloved Sweetfern Harbor, Sweet Peach Bakery, and Alaska Cozy series. Wendy calls New Hampshire home, where she lives with her husband, two sons, two mini pigs who have big personalities, and an adorable Labradoodle who rules the roost.

Visit her website at www.wendymeadows.com for latest releases, discounts and more!

amazon.com/author/wendymeadows

bookbub.com/profile/wendy-meadows

goodreads.com/wendymeadows